Treasure of San Miguel

During the war with Mexico, many of the rich towns and monasteries had been looted and the treasures taken north. Some, though, had been hurriedly buried by their owners, their hiding places lost over the years. Marshal Ben Littlejohn first came into contact with the treasure of San Miguel when investigating the mysterious shooting of an old cowhand.

The last person to see the old man alive had been Carrico Manvell, a whiplash of a man, smartly dressed, dark-skinned with thin lips, eyes as hard as agate, and a record of killings that stretched back across half a dozen states.

Rumour in El Angelo had it that the cowhand had an authentic map giving the location of the San Miguel treasure, but Littlejohn accepted this information with caution. Such maps were a dime a dozen, completely valueless and sold to gullible visitors along the Mexican border.

But for once, the rumours proved to be well-founded and that was when the killing really began.

Treasure of San Miguel

Dean Layton

A Black Horse Western

ROBERT HALE · LONDON

© 1966, 2003 John Glasby
First hardcover edition 2003
Originally published in paperback as
The Rawhide Ones by Chuck Adams

ISBN 0 7090 7250 3

Robert Hale Limited
Clerkenwell House
Clerkenwell Green
London EC1R 0HT

Typeset by
Derek Doyle & Associates, Liverpool.
Printed and bound in Great Britain by
Antony Rowe Limited, Wiltshire

ONE

THE GUNHAWKS

The thick overcast which had blotted out all sight of the sun all day had cleared during the late evening and a moon was showing above the mountain rim to the east as Ben Littlejohn put his mount to the downgrade, sitting forward a little in the saddle, legs braced hard against the stirrups as the horse slid on its haunches for a little way, the loose treacherous shale giving way under its forelegs. The dark bulk of the trees, most of it first-year pine, loomed ahead of him against the clearing heavens.

He had ridden hard for almost two days, sleeping only for four or five hours during the night, travelling fast. This was new country to him, but he felt no concern. He had been born and raised in the mountains of Wyoming, knew how to make himself at home wherever the night found him. The country just north of the Texas border with Mexico was reputed to be clear of Indians now, but there was no guarantee of it and he rode with his ears cocked for the faintest sound, his hand never straying very far from the butt of the revolver at his hip. Men who ventured off the main trails in this territory did so at their own risk.

Reaching the bottom of the rocky incline, he rode for a

5

short distance until the trail led him up to the crest of a high knoll, then reined up, scanning the country ahead. There were hordes of little creeping shadows lying across the trail, thrown by moon and starlight and the tricky, shifting overtones of light and shade placed a moving figure at the back of every bush and tree, endowing the pines with an oddly human form. Digging into his pocket, he pulled out the makings of a smoke, rolled the cigarette expertly in his fingers, thrust it between his lips and lit it, drawing the smoke down into his lungs, letting it trickle out through his nostrils.

For a long moment he sat there, letting the long seconds pile up. Somewhere ahead of him lay the small town of El Angelo, just across the mountains, ten miles inside the border of Texas. He had never been to this place before, had never laid eyes on any of the citizens of El Angelo except perhaps one. The letter in his pocket had reached him three weeks before in Denver. The envelope bore only his name and it was impossible to guess how long it had taken to find him.

Finishing his smoke, he tossed the butt into the moist grass beside the trail, pulled the letter from his pocket and drew out the worn and dirty single sheet of paper. Holding it close, he read through it, making out only a few words in the moonlight that filtered down through the trees, but having read it so often before that he knew it by heart:

Dear Ben,
It's now seven years since we were last together and I offered you a partnership in the ranch, which you turned down to become a lawman. Since then I've heard nothing from you, although I've heard a lot about you, Abilene, Devil's Creek, Denver. I have no idea whether you are still in Denver, so I am mailing this letter there in the hope that it will somehow find you and before it is too late.

You always said that if there was any favour I ever wanted of you, I was to write at once. Knowing how troublesome these frontier towns can be, I have been reluctant to do so, but things are very bad in El Angelo these days. Cattle are being rustled almost every night and there is no law and order, no one to keep these outlaws in check. Daily they are becoming more and more arrogant, even to riding into town, holding the ranchers to ransom. There is somebody behind them, planning all of their moves, somebody big, but although we have our suspicions, we can prove nothing. If you should receive this letter and can see your way clear to ride down to the border for a visit, however short it may be, be careful. These men can tell a lawman a mile away and they will go to extreme lengths to see that you meet with an unfortunate accident on the trail.

> Sincerely yours,
> Andrew Faulds

Folding the letter carefully, he replaced it in the envelope and thrust it back into his pocket. His face betrayed little of the worry he felt in his mind. In the seven years of which Andrew had written, he had drifted from one hell-town to another, an empty, cold man, with no spark of warmth in him. That was, he figured, one of the penalties that a man paid for being a lawman. There were always the law-abiding citizens on one side of you, squeezing you hard against the lawless breed. If you shot down a man in the dusty street of one of these frontier towns, there were those who censured you for it, even though they knew, deep down inside, that you had done the only right thing, the thing they paid you for.

He twitched his lips in a wry smile. As time went on, the chances of being killed, of meeting the man who was faster with a gun than he was himself, were doubling all of the time. And added to this was the inevitable fact that when the showdown came, the solid citizens of the town would, in all probability, refuse to back him against the lawless. He had the feeling it would be the same in El Angelo judging from what Faulds had written. But eight years before, Faulds had saved his life and he still owed him that favour, one which he was determined to repay.

He had ridden steadily for five days now, crossing desertland covered with the sharp-smelling, bitter sage and few waterholes. A land where little could live, the dry vegetation which managed to suck a precarious existence out of the dry, acid soil, rattling like bleached bones in the ceaseless wind. Then, on the southern edge of the desert, he had reached the high country, the tall range of mountains, taking the winding, narrow trail which led up to the summit through the pines and cedars, riding across the swift-moving watercourses that raced down the rocky ledges. He had met no one on the trail although he knew from past experience that these hills were far from empty. Men lived here, well away from the trails, in tiny wooden shacks and cabins, set back in the difficult country, close to water, where they could be alone. The great majority of these men were on the run from the law, wanted in some state or other, willing to stand the silence, the isolation and the monotony of this country so that they might stay alive. Tired of running endlessly with the chance of a bullet at the end of it, they simply pulled away from the world, living off the land.

It was not the best sort of country for a man with a star and Ben had kept away from the tiny, half-seen trails that wound up into the thicker vegetation whenever he had smelled woodsmoke, even though there might have been the chance of a meal at the end.

Now, with the round yellow face of the moon lifting over the topmost branches of the trees, he had reached the spot where the trail took its downward turn. Gigging his mount forward slowly, he found a place where a narrow stream had forced a path through the clinging brush and here he turned off the trail, moved back for twenty yards or so, dismounting in a small clearing, well hidden from the trail by the thick wall of vegetation.

Building a fire, he ate a quick meal, drank the hot coffee, then settled his back against a tree stump and smoked a cigarette contentedly, forcing the nagging worry from his mind. Another day would see him in El Angelo and once he met Faulds again, he would be able to discover what was troubling the other, maybe do something about it himself. Finishing his smoke, he put his horse on picket in a small flat of grass just beyond the rim of firelight, then dragged his blankets out close by and watched the dark patch of the night sky where the canopy of leaves and branches overhead thinned out. The stars swirled above him in a glory of diamond constellations, dimming a little close to the full moon that rode high and cold above the trees. At this elevation, there was still a small, cool wind that sighed down the mountain slopes from the topmost crests and he drew his blanket more tightly about him, turning a little into a comfortable position.

It was still dark when he woke, jerked swiftly into awareness by the run of a horse far down along the trail. Reaching out, he tossed a handful of earth onto the faintly glowing embers, listening to the oncoming horse for a moment, judging its distance. It could be that the smoke from his fire would give his presence away to the rider but he doubted it. The wind was blowing it back into the undergrowth away from the trail. Interest and caution rose together in him as he eased himself silently out of his blankets, moved the Colt slowly in its holster once or twice and crouched waiting, straining to listen, to separate fantasy from fact.

Whoever the rider was, he seemed in an all-fired hurry, pushing his mount upgrade at a fast run. The sound drew level with Ben, then passed on without faltering. He remained quite still, listening to the scrubbing abrasion of hoofs moving into the distance again. Then, abruptly, they stopped.

Ben waited. The sounds did not continue. *Somehow, he smelled the smoke,* he thought tensely. *That's why he's stopped. Now he'll be moving around, circling the trail to move in and take a look see.*

He turned towards the fire and moved up, now in more of a hurry than he had been. The fire was out when he reached it, the earth having damped it completely. There was the faint smell of smoke persisting in the air, but there was nothing he could do about that now. Gently, leaving his horse where it could be readily seen, he eased back into the bushes, crouched down, his gun out, finger on the trigger.

It was almost five minutes later when he heard the noise of someone approaching from the thick brush behind the clearing. Starlight made a faint, trembling glow on the branches that swayed a little in the wind and there seemed to be far too many shadows around in which a man might hide. The faint crackle of a twig snapping underfoot came to him out of the gloom and afterwards he heard the soft rattling of a dry-branched bush. All this was beyond the clearing, ahead of him, beyond sight. The noise in the undergrowth ceased for a while as if the other man was a little unsure of himself now, had guessed that the camp was close by but was not certain whether or not he had been heard. He must have guessed that the sound of his horse would have awoken anyone when he had ridden by on the trail and this was, perhaps, making him doubly cautious.

Ben paused for a moment to debate the proposition. He recalled what Andrew Faulds had said in his letter, that if anyone in El Angelo got to hear of his coming, they might do everything in their power to prevent him from getting there.

Was this, maybe, their way of doing it? Sending out men to

scour the trail, watching for strangers, bushwhacking them on the way? He had met up with something like this on several occasions in the past. A man did not hold down a lawman's job for six years without meeting every kind of killer and he knew that the bushwhackers were the worst and most dangerous kind. They killed without any danger to themselves, shooting a man in the back from cover, giving him no chance to go for his gun.

A faint rustle in the brush on the far side of the clearing attracted his attention a moment later and peering into the starlight, he saw a dark shape move forward in a half crouch. The shimmering light glinted off the barrel of a drawn gun. Ben watched as the man moved around the rim of bushes, then pause as he caught sight of the horse standing patiently on the grass bank. Turning, the other edged towards the blankets, just visible in the dimness. Ben let him get within five feet of them, saw the downward tilt of the gun in the man's hand, then said sharply: 'Hold it right there mister and drop that gun.'

The other's head snapped up with a jerk. For a second, he pointed his gun tightly in his hand, the thought of using it visible in the poised outline of his body, the slightly hunched shoulders.

'Drop it, I said!'

There was the muffled crash of a gun falling into the brush. Slowly, the man stepped away towards the centre of the clearing, his hands held away from his sides.

Getting to his feet, Ben walked forward. He held his gun steady, his eyes cold and hard as tempered steel, his face grim set. Presently, he said softly: 'Mister, I guess you know I'd be well within my rights to shoot you down right now.'

There was a pause, then the other said in a tight voice: 'Could be that we've got this thing all wrong, mister.'

'How do you savvy that?' Ben asked quietly.

'You wouldn't be Ben Littlejohn, would you?'

The question took Ben by surprise. He narrowed his eyes a shade. If the other man had been sent out to kill him, it was unlikely he would ask his identity as directly as this.

Something wasn't right here, he thought. As he recalled Faulds' letter, he had warned him of possible trouble. This could be it. Caution took a hold of him. He edged back slightly, still covering the other with his gun. He did not recognize the man at all.

'Sometimes it doesn't do to ask questions.'

'If you are Ben Littlejohn, then you're the man I'm looking for. Andrew Faulds asked me to keep a sharp look out for you. I was to warn you that you're riding into trouble, big trouble, in El Angelo.'

'I know that much already.' Ben said. 'You looked to me as though you meant to bushwhack me. That gun you had in your hand wasn't just for show.'

'I had to be sure who you were.' The other hesitated, then went on: 'This is one hell of a stretch of territory. You don't know the half of it.' He paused, then said probingly: 'You ain't said yet whether you're Littlejohn.'

'I'm Littlejohn,' Ben said. 'But why should you be ridin' the trail lookin' for me? Why did Faulds have to send you?'

'Why couldn't he come for himself, you mean,' said the other softly. He had turned to face Ben now. His tone implied that Ben's question made him a fool for asking it. 'I'll tell you. I'll tell you how close you are to being a dead man if you persist in ridin' on into El Angelo. I don't know you, Littlejohn. But I've been a close friend of Andrew's for the past four years. He's the only one who dared to offer me a job when Manvell tried to run me out of town. That's one of the reasons why Manvell has sworn to kill Faulds.'

'So he sent you to warn me?'

'That's right. He'd have come himself, only there was some trouble a week or so ago.'

'What sort of trouble?' Ben felt tension building up inside

him. The other's story held a certain ring of truth, but he was still not absolutely satisfied with it.

'Faulds took a bunch of his boys out onto the range to keep an eye on the herd. Plenty of his cattle have been rustled in the past and he figured that it was time he stopped it, forced a showdown with the rustlers. There was a gunfight and he stopped a bullet in the shoulder, nicked one of his ribs. He's laid up right now, otherwise he would probably have come himself.'

This time, Ben believed him. He let the Colt fall back into its holster, nodding. 'All right, mister, pick up your gun.'

The other bent, picked up his gun and slipped it back into leather. Straightening, he said: 'Like I told you, I work for Faulds. The name's Lander.'

Ben nodded, then shrugged, studying the other closely in the filtering of moonlight that reached the clearing through the trees. The man was quite tall and heavily-built, with a high-bridged nose and sharp eyes that now fastened a plainly appraising glance on Ben.

Presently, he said: 'Do you reckon that you'll be good enough to stop Carrico Manvell and his men, Littlejohn? I reckon I'd better warn you that in the past a lot of good men have tried it – and failed. Most of 'em are buried in the cemetery overlooking El Angelo.'

'I figure we won't know that until Manvell puts in his chips and we find out,' Ben said quietly. He sat down near the dead embers of the fire, watched as the other whistled up his mount. Then he said: 'This needs a little explainin'. Why should Faulds write me a letter askin' me to come as fast as I could, and then send you out here to warn me off?'

Lander pursed his lips, stared down at his hands resting on his knees. 'I guess you'd better ask him when you see him.' He lifted his head, laid his level gaze on Ben. 'You are still meanin' to ride on into El Angelo, aren't you?'

'That's right. I've never backed away from trouble yet. I

avoid it if I can, but when it's inevitable, then the only way is to go out and meet it, never to wait until it comes to you.'

'I must say that you're a cool one,' murmured the other. 'Faulds said that you wouldn't scare easy. He figured that Manvell would get to know somehow that he had sent for you and that there'd be a reception committee waitin' for you in town, or someplace along the trail. That's why he asked me to warn you.'

'Things seem to have changed in El Angelo since this *hombre* Manvell tried to take over. Last time I heard from Faulds, he was doin' well on the ranch.'

'Nobody knows where Manvell came from originally. He rode into town one day a couple of years back, bought himself a few head of beef and took over the old Triple C ranch. Since then, he's built it up into one of the biggest spreads in the territory. We're pretty certain that most of the cattle he has now were rustled from neighbouring herds, but nobody can prove that and anybody rash enough to say so out loud, is either run out of the town or dies in mysterious circumstances.'

'Now hold on,' Ben said. 'Why don't the ranchers band together and run him out of the territory?'

'Don't let any talk you might hear about Carrico Manvell fool you.' Lander rested back against the trunk of a tree, letting his arms hang loose across his legs. He relaxed as though he had previously been under a strain. Patting his shirt pocket, he brought out a cigar, thrust it between his lips and lighted it, closing his eyes for a moment; then he opened them, fixing his gaze keenly and sharply on Ben. 'Manvell is a cold-blooded killer. Not the ordinary run of gunman you meet in this frontier territory. He has men working for him, all gunhawks who like nothin' better than to shoot up the men workin' on the small ranches. It's hard for the ranchers to get anyone to work for them now. Even in the town, nobody dare go against Manvell. There's no law and order, except his.'

'But Faulds stood up against him all this time.'

'Sure.' There was a trace of bitterness edging the other's voice now, and his fingers, intertwined, tightened abruptly, the knuckles standing out white under the flesh, 'But how long will he be able to keep up the fight? A bullet in his shoulder, grazing a rib. The next time, it could be through his heart.'

While the other stretched himself out on the ground at the edge of the clearing, his even breathing telling Ben that he had fallen asleep, Littlejohn sat smoking, staring off into the darkness that lay all around him. All he could see ahead of him was trouble and he would be inevitably caught in the middle of it. But the point was that it had now become a personal thing with him. He had not imagined it was as bad as this, when he had first received Andrew's letter and set out from Denver, but from what Lander had told him, there could be the makings of a full scale range war brewing up around El Angelo. He would have liked to have made plans for when he rode into this town, but things were happening a little too fast for that. The feeling that events were being thrust on him, were getting out of his control, was growing stronger in his mind.

The two men saddled up and rode out of the clearing just as an early dawn was streaking the eastern horizon with pale channels of grey. The last of the stars still shone low in the west close to where the round face of the moon was dipping behind the lowermost ridges. Halfway along the gorge leading down to the valley, the ledge road wound along the edge of the river below them. Ben leaned sideways in his saddle, stared down at the rushing water as it splashed over the rough, stony bottom. It was the dry season now and the river was running low, but he guessed that once the spring rains fell, it would become a raging, swollen monster, something to be reckoned with, and anybody riding down this stretch of the trail after dark, did so at his own risk.

As he rode, he thought about Andrew Faulds. He could not see a good motive for anyone wanting to run off all of the cattle from the range, unless Manvell intended taking over the entire territory. But there was, of course, much he did not know, things he would have to find out for himself by careful questioning. He wondered if anybody apart from Faulds would talk freely to him, especially if they learned who he was and why he happened to be there.

Half an hour later, they swung down from the looming heights of the mountains, cut over a narrow wooden bridge which spanned the river, the trail twisting tortuously before they rode out onto the plains which stretched as far as the eye could see, clear to the Mexican border.

Riding beside him, he noticed Lander fidgeting nervously the saddle, his eyes switching continually from one side to the other. He was ill-at-ease, clearly anticipating trouble, not sure from which direction it would come.

'You figure they may try to jump us before we get to town?' he asked suddenly.

'If they reckon they can get away with it, they will,' grunted the other. 'I feel it in my bones. They're around here some-place.'

'Not many places where they could dry gulch us here,' Ben commented. He glanced about him. The bright sun had lifted now, changing the early morning chill into a flat, breathless heat that lay over everything, touching the whole scene with a harsh yellow glare that was hurting to the eyes.

They kept to the rolling country on the edge of the wide plains, still taking all of the proper precautions against a sudden attack. For more than two miles, neither man spoke, Lander still uneasy at his own fears of a bullet out of the silent wastes on either side of them. They topped a rise overlooking the sluggish river where it flowed wider here than it had in the canyon, rode parallel with it for a while, then cut down past a wide basin, over a stretch of smoother country and finally came in sight of El Angelo, a dark smudge on the distant horizon.

As they rode towards it, Lander pointed off to their right. 'Yonder is the Triple C ranch. That trail will lead you right to it.'

'And Fauld's spread?'

'Beyond the town, to the south. Used to be a real big place, more'n five thousand head of the best beef cattle. Less than a fifth of that left now. And with nobody carin' to work for him, I don't see how he's goin' to keep on. He'll be forced to sell out to Manvell and lose nearly everything he's built up for himself.'

Ben nodded, said nothing more. His face was grim and set as he sat forward in the saddle, eyes staring bleakly ahead.

Glancing sideways at him, Lander found himself wondering a little about this man. Maybe he had been wrong about him, he thought; maybe he was just the man to end the reign of terror which Carrico Manvell had begun around El Angelo.

They rode steadily and gradually the individual buildings of the town showed clearly through the shimmering heat haze that enveloped the land. Ben rode with narrowed eyes. Most of the land to the north of the town was alkali, with no grass to feed animals. Clearly there were only a few patches of good earth which would grow the grass to support the herds of beef cattle.

An hour later, they entered El Angelo. The main street was a wide and dusty thoroughfare that ran straight as an arrow through the middle of the town, with narrower alleys running into it from either side. Most of the buildings were of adobe style, reflecting the southern tastes just across the border in Mexico. There were a few, mostly on the northern outskirts which had been built around the time of Spanish colonialism, luxurious in their heyday, but now falling into ruin and disrepair. Only one, set back from the road, still bore traces

17

of its earlier glory. It bore the faded sign: Trail's End Saloon over the wide door. On the narrow boardwalk which fronted the saloon, several men sat back in chairs, basking in the welcome shade of the overhang, watching the two men closely and with a sharpened interest as they rode slowly by.

They passed a stable, horses visible in the darkened interior, a white-whiskered man leaning on a broom eyeing them curiously while trying to appear disinterested.

Then there were some vacant, weed-covered lots until the hotel, a two-storied building stood next door to the bank which edged close on to the Sheriff's Office. Out of the corner of his eye, Ben noticed the lack of paint on the office door and the thick layer of dust which overlaid on the street window. He felt a grim amusement course through him. Evidently Lander had not been exaggerating when he had claimed there was no law and order in El Angelo.

'Be careful,' Lander said softly out of the corner of his mouth. 'When they see you with me they'll know who you are. They may decide to make their play here in town or wait until we ride out to the ranch.'

Ben nodded. All of these years as a lawman had taught him what signs to watch out for when riding through an uneasy town such as this. He could read a great many things in the way the townsfolk watched him covertly from beneath lowered lids. If they guessed he was a lawman, they gave no outward sign, but they obviously read him as someone capable of making trouble. Apart from the man who rode beside him, there was no way he had of distinguishing friend from foe here. The letter from Faulds had given him plenty of cause for concern so, as a matter of habit, he gave every man he saw the same careful appraisal. Often that was enough to determine whether a man would make a play for him or not.

When they were almost opposite the low-roofed saloon halfway along the street, he noticed the man standing with his shoulders leaning against one of the wooden uprights, thumbs thrust into his belt. Ben saw that the other was young, probably in his early twenties. He stood evenly balanced on the balls of his feet, his gaze fixed firmly on Ben's face, gaze locking with his. There was something resembling a faint sneer on his slightly handsome features. He stood there for a long moment, as though wanting to make himself seen by the lawman. Then he turned deliberately and slowly on his heel and walked into the saloon, pushing the doors open with the flat of his left hand. Even at that distance, there was something about him which Ben had seen many times before with other men, something he recognized instantly. The kid carried himself with an arrogant certainty, utterly sure of himself, the gun at his waist holstered low on his thigh, the black butt polished smooth by long use, tied tightly in its place. Evidently the man who believed that his life hung on the speed of his draw.

Ben twisted his lips a little wryly. He could not mistake the other's brand. There were all sorts of gunhawks. Those who killed because they were paid to do so and thought nothing of their reputation so long as they killed and received their money. They would shoot a man in the back without warning. Then there were the others who thought more of building up a reputation as a gunslinger than earning blood money. These men were always looking for trouble, confident that they were faster than the man they challenged, giving the other the benefit of the draw, believing that this enhanced their reputation. He guessed that the kid who had just gone into the saloon was one of this kind. He may have been paid to cause trouble by Manvell. But he would not call Ben out just for that. It would be a matter of pride.

If Ben was guessing this situation right, he had two choices open to him. To go into the saloon right now, face the other down and have it out with him there and then. Or he could wait and play the case slow and easy, wait for the other to make his move. There was the possibility that he had read the other's brand wrong and had misjudged him; but somehow he did not think so.

Lander had noticed the direction of his glance. Now he said very softly: 'That was Ed Fazer. He's a real bad one. Works for Manvell. I've heard tell that he's real lightning with a gun.'

Ben raised his gaze to the other's face. 'You reckon he's here to make trouble for me?'

'Could be.' There was a faint note of anxiety in the other's tone. 'You saw the way he carries his gun.'

'Sure, I noticed it all right. But a man can carry a gun like that and still be slow using it.'

'I wouldn't count on it,' muttered the other. 'This is a real hell town. You want to ride on out to Fauld's place?'

Ben shook his head. 'I reckon I could do with a drink to wash the trail dust out of my throat.' He reined up his mount, slid from the saddle, and threw the reins over the hitching rail, stepping up onto the boardwalk, waiting for the other to step down. For a moment, Lander stared down at him in surprise, then he got down. He let out a long, audible sigh.

'This could be just what Manvell wants. Get you out of the way before you can start probing around.'

'Maybe,' Ben said curtly. 'Let's find out. The only way to meet trouble if it is coming for you, is head on. No sense in lettin' it sneak up on you from behind.'

He pushed open the batwing doors, stepped into the coolness of the saloon. There were a few men already there, some playing at faro at one of the tables, others standing at the bar. For a moment, Ben held a batwing in each hand. Then he stood aside for Lander to go in, let the doors go and they began to swing and creak behind him as he made his way slowly across to the bar, moving in easy, casual steps.

Lifting his finger Ben laid his elbows on the bar, resting his weight on them. The barkeep hesitated, then idled over. He stared at Ben for a moment, then flickered a glance at Lander.

'This *hombre* with you, Lander?'

'That's right.'

'From the way you talk, you sound as though you want to make somethin' of it,' Ben said ominously.

The other stared at him silently for a long moment and could see him growing smaller and smaller with every second that passed. Then the man craw-fished. 'Don't mean nothin' mister. Just don't like strangers too much around here. Been too much trouble already.'

'I don't aim to start any trouble. But if it comes, I'm ready to meet it,' Ben said evenly. 'Seems there's plenty of lawlessness in this town.'

There was a faint snigger from along the bar. Ben turned his head slowly and stared across at the kid who stood half facing him. The sneer was clearly visible on his face now, 'Heard tell you might be on your way here,' he said thinly. He swept his gaze around the saloon. 'This here is Marshal Ben Littlejohn. Guess you boys have all heard of him. A fast man with a gun. They say he cleaned up Devil's Creek and Denver.' The beat of sarcasm was clearly audible in the other's tone. 'I allow that he ain't so fast as folk say. That right, Marshal?'

Ben stiffened, then forced himself to relax. He knew the other was now deliberately taunting him, trying to force a showdown. He was not afraid of meeting it, but he would prefer to know the reason behind this first.

'Seems to me you've got somethin' on your mind, mister,' he said slowly. 'I'd like to know what it is.'

The other grinned, did not move. 'You could say I don't hold with lawmen sneaking into town, not totin' a badge to let folk know their intentions. They say that Faulds sent for you.'

'That's right,' Ben nodded. 'Looks to me that its got nothin' to do with you. Unless you're figurin on tryin' to stop me.'

21

The smile vanished from the other's face. His eyes narrowed a shade and Ben saw the killer look cross his face, the crazy look that Ben had seen on the faces of other gun toters so often before. 'Now that just might be my intention, Littlejohn.'

It had been quiet in the saloon before this, but suddenly it was deathly still. Fazer had spoken softly, but his words carried to every corner of the room.

Ben said equally softly: 'You're makin a big mistake, Fazer. You see, I know somethin' about you too. You're a gunslinger who the law never caught up with. You got bored a couple of years back, joined forces with Manvell, hirin' out your gun to him. Could be you figured that he'd shield you in case the law ever did show up. I guess that business has been pretty good ever since; but all good things have to come to an end.'

From behind the bar, the barkeep said jerkily: 'I reckon you'd better leave, Marshal. You're way out of your territory here and I don't figure on gettin' the place shot up and that's just where this kind of talk leads.'

'Sorry, mister, but I'm afraid I can't oblige you there,' Ben said evenly. 'Seems to me that *hombre* is lookin' for trouble and he ain't goin' to stop just because you say so. Besides, I got the feelin' you might be inclined to use that sawn-off shotgun you've got stacked away just behind the bar yonder.' Ben did not turn his attention away from Fazer as he spoke, but he sensed the astonished look on the barkeep's face, saw him step back slightly, away from the spot where the scattergun was obviously deposited. He knew that the man would now make no attempt to use it. The other was the type of man who had seen very little trouble in the saloon since Manvell had taken over. Evidently his customers here were mostly the gunhawks who worked for Manvell and the other would keep a tight rein on the men he hired. The owlhoots who frequented this place were all on the run from the law, seeking a place to hide and there would be the usual mutual agreement among them to solve any personal feuds they might have elsewhere.

'Then you'd better back down, Ed.' The other turned to Fazer. 'I don't want no trouble here and—'

'Guess you've forgotten already,' said Fazer softly. 'Manvell said this lawman wasn't to get to Faulds. Don't say how he was to be stopped and if I prefer it this way, reckon you'd better keep your mouth shut.'

Angry now, the barkeep slammed a glass to the bar, tucked the moist cloth into his belt and moved away, down the bar to the far end, out of the way of any bullets that might start flying.

Turning now to face Fazer, Ben felt quite calm and still inwardly. 'All right, Fazer,' he said evenly, 'you've spoken your piece. Carrico Manvell paid you to kill me. Then let's see you earn your blood money.' As he spoke, he watched the rest of the men in the room with unfocused stare, taking in everything in a single glance without once removing his attention from Fazer. He saw the men at the card tables and further along the bar, although watching closely, were not preparing to take any part in this affair. This was just between him and Ed Fazer.

Fazer smiled thinly, edged away from the bar, his hand swinging slowly by his side. He moved forward a little until he was standing less than eight feet from Ben. Standing relaxed, he gave a slight nod, his fingers rubbing together close to his belt buckle, eyes narrowed again. At this distance, it was impossible for either man to miss and everything now would depend on speed.

'You were a fool to take any notice of that letter Faulds sent, Littlejohn,' Fazer said. He made to go on speaking, but it was just a feint to distract Ben's attention from what he meant to do and the lawman ignored him, said curtly:

'Manvell paid you money to kill me, Fazer. What are you waitin' for? Your courage soaked out through the soles of your boots?'

The barb struck home. He saw the other's handsome face flush angrily, saw his lips tighten into a hard line, the fingers of his gunhand twitched a little above the butt of the gun. He stood rigid, then ran the tip of his tongue around lips which seemed to have suddenly turned dry. It was quite a while since he had stacked up against a man of Ben Littlejohn's calibre and he was becoming a little more unsure of himself.

Ben let the long seconds pile up, smiling a little at the other. It was a trick he had learned from past experience, the sure mark of confidence for a gunman. If the other man felt you were dead sure, it sapped his own courage, made him just that shade slower when it came to the showdown, let his nerves tighten up inside him until they were stretched to breaking point.

Fazer crouched slightly, his right shoulder dropping to get the edge, right hand hooked like a claw. His eyes never left Ben's face.

'All right, Littlejohn, jerk your iron,' snarled the other.

Ben shook his head slowly. 'This is your play, Fazer,' he said. There was no trace of emotion in his voice. He saw the gunhawk's hand tremble for a second above his gunbutt. Then it sped downward, fingers opening, closing around the smooth walnut of the Colt.

He was in the act of jerking it from the holster when Ben's hand moved downward with the speed of a striking snake, lifting his Colt from leather, levelling it, and squeezing the trigger in a single, fluid motion. The bullet hit Fazer in the chest, high up and the men in the saloon saw the gunhawk reel backward as the heavy slug pitched him against one of the tables that fell and smashed beneath his weight as he went down. A nervous, instinctive spasm of his finger put a pressure on the trigger and the bullet ploughed into one of the lamps hanging above the bar, splinters of glass cascading onto the floor. Ben walked towards the other through the smoke haze, the barrel of his gun lowered to cover the gunhawk, but

24

even as he reached him, the gun dropped from Fazer's nerve-less fingers and his head fell back onto the floor with a dull thud, blood trickling from his open mouth.

Ben stood and thumbed a shell into his six-gun, then turned to eye the rest of the men in the saloon. He noticed the way their eyes fell whenever he stared at them. The barkeep leaned forward over the counter, his eyes popping.

'You beat Ed Fazer to the draw.' he said in a half-whisper.

Without replying to him, Ben moved back to the bar and picked up his drink, tossed it down in a single gulp. He had done all he could to avoid having to kill the other man, but it had not been enough. From what Faulds had said in his letter and what he had later heard from Lander, this was not the end, but the beginning of the trouble for him in El Angelo. He knew inwardly that he could not back out now, that his course was set and he had no recourse but to go on.

Turning back to the barkeep he said in a thin tone: 'You'd better get him out of here and send word to the coroner.' In the mirror behind the bar, he noticed the thin, weasel-faced man who had got silently to his feet and was edging towards the door.

Swinging lightly on his feet, he said: 'You goin' out to tell Manvell that his gunhawk is dead, mister?'

The man stopped in mid-stride. His face was hard set and stubborn. 'Figure he ought to know, Marshal,' he said hesi-tantly.

Ben nodded, took one step forward. 'Better tell him too, that even if this town ain't got any law and order, it's sure goin' to have justice.'

TWO

GUN HIGH

Cal Mentor reached the Triple C ranch sometime before dark, put his horse away in the livery stable and made his way along to the house, stepping up onto the porch just as the door opened and Carrico Manvell came out. He was the kind of man you looked at and after you had turned away, glanced back to look again. He was thin, lean-hipped, with lazy eyes that were nevertheless bold and roamed every place, taking in all that was going on in a single, unblinking stare.

He asked shortly 'Littlejohn show up in town?'

'He's here,' Mentor said harshly. 'Rode in a few hours ago. Came with Lander, Fauld's foreman.'

'Did Fazer kill him like I said?'

'No.'

Manvell shot him a bright-sharp glance. His lips twisted for a moment into an expression of anger, but when he spoke his voice was perfectly controlled. 'Why not? What happened in town?'

'Fazer called him in the saloon. Littlejohn beat him to the draw and shot him down. It was a fair fight, Fazer drew first and—'

'I'm not interested in whether it was a fair fight or not,' Manvell snapped. He turned, then gestured towards the house. 'Come inside. There's somethin' I want to talk to you about.'

He led the way inside, closing the door. Mentor felt a little self-conscious as he stood in the parlour of the house, blinking at the lantern on the table. Manvell walked around the heavy oak table, lowered himself into a chair, then placed the tips of his slim fingers together and stared over them at the other.

'You know why Faulds sent for Littlejohn, I suppose?'

'To fight you and the Triple C.'

'That's right. I don't aim to sit here and wait for this jumped-up lawman to start any big trouble with me.'

'He's lightning fast with a gun,' affirmed the other. 'Never saw a man as fast. After what happened to Ed, you won't get many men to go up against him.'

'There are other ways of gettin' rid of him than calling him out like Fazer did. He was a goddamned fool. He could've killed him without exposing himself to any danger, but he had that stiff-necked pride that made him think he was the fastest gun in the territory. Now he's dead and Littlejohn is still alive.'

'You want me to get hold of some of the boys and head out the Faulds' place? If we were to cut over the hills we could reach there before he does.'

'No,' Manvell's tone was sharp. 'I'll take care of Littlejohn in my own good time and my own way. I've somethin' else for you to do. And I don't want this job bungled, you understand?'

'Sure, boss,' Mentor nodded quickly. At the moment, he could see nothing more urgent or important than getting Littlejohn off their backs, but he knew that Manvell had something on his mind, otherwise he would not have delayed in getting rid of this lawman. Ordinarily, Manvell was a reasonable man, easy enough to get along with so long as he wasn't crossed and things were going his way. Very few people dared to cross him now. In the few years that he had been here, he had built up an empire for himself that more than matched anything else around El Angelo. Only Faulds had dared to oppose him and if it hadn't been for the intervention of this marshal, things might have reached a satisfactory conclusion very soon. Now Mentor wasn't quite so sure. In the two years he had worked for Manvell he had seen the hatred for Faulds grow into something so big that it was a gnawing poison in him now.

But when Manvell spoke again, it was not about Faulds, or Littlejohn. He leaned back in his chair, said softly: 'You know this old fool Monroe who sometimes rides into town from the hills?'

'Charlie Monroe? Sure, everybody knows him,' Mentor's face wrinkled in a look of surprise. 'You interested in him?'

Manvell nodded slowly. 'I've been hearin' some interestin' gossip about Monroe. They say he has a map showing where the treasure of San Miguel was buried fifty years or more ago. There's gold and silver worth more than a quarter of a million dollars buried somewhere in the hills and if this old coot knows where it is, then I mean to have it. I want you to keep an eye on the trails, let me know as soon as Monroe rides back into El Angelo.'

'You really believe that story?' Mentor asked.

'All I know is that the gold and silver plate was taken from the monastery of San Miguel just over the border from here and buried so that the Yankees didn't get their hands on it. If they meant to go back and get it sometime, then there'd be a map of its whereabouts.'

'But why do you think that Monroe has it? If there's any truth in these rumours, why hasn't he gone out to get it for himself?'

Manvell shrugged. 'How should I know what goes on in that crazy mind of his? Maybe he doesn't realize what he's got. Maybe he doesn't even believe in it himself? Could be that he's tried to find it without any success. I'm not interested in the reasons. All I'm interested in is gettin' my hands on that map. Once I see it, I'll know whether or not it's genuine.'

'So I just keep an eye on the trails. You don't want me to stop Monroe and get that map for you?'

'No!' Manvell said with emphasis. 'You just let me know when he rides back. I'll take care of the rest. I know the place where he puts up when he's in town.'

'Sure thing,' Mentor nodded. He turned and went out, moving slowly over to the bunkhouse. The night wind held a cold touch and he pulled the collar of his jacket higher around his neck. Lying in his bunk, he stared up at the ceiling over his head in the darkness, only half aware of the sounds of the other sleeping men in the bunkhouse. As he lay there, his thoughts fastened on what Manvell had told him. Could there be any truth in this gossip of a map showing where that treasure was hidden?

He had heard other men talk of the treasure of San Miguel. The Spanish monasteries had been fabulously rich and those who had been unable to transport their wealth south during the bitter fighting between Spain and America had hidden it in the hills, maybe believing that Spain would win the war and they would then have an opportunity to go back for it. But when America had taken over Texas, their chance was gone and the treasure was, as far as anybody knew, still where it had been buried by those men almost fifty years before.

Turning over on his side, he pushed the thought of gold out of his head. Even if Manvell was right about that map which Charlie Monroe was supposed to carry with him, there would be none of it for him. Manvell was too smart to let any man put one over on him. He'd grab off all that wealth for himself if he ever found it.

Back in the ranch-house, Carrico Manvell continued to sit

at the table long after Mentor's footsteps had faded across the yard outside. The little imp of avarice in his brain kept murmuring to him: *Get the map and then go out for that gold. It's out there someplace.*

A tense eagerness took hold of him. The gold hunger in his brain was stronger for a moment than the knowledge that there was a further threat to him in El Angelo. This was the kind of situation that Manvell found interesting. He drew unhurriedly on his smoke. Already his mind was busy turning over the various possibilities which suggested themselves. He had a lot here in El Angelo, there was no doubting that. A few short years and he owned most of the land north of the Rio Grande. Only Faulds was still holding out against him; and he intended to rid himself of this obstacle very soon. But there were other things crowding his mind which would have to be taken care of; besides, he did not believe that Littlejohn intended to make any real trouble as yet. Maybe if Faulds succeeded in talking him into something he might, but until that moment, Manvell was prepared to take things as they came.

Rising finally to his feet, he leaned over the table and extinguished the lamp by drawing his cupped hand sharply over the top of it.

Lander led the way across a vast depression where the crowding rocky gulches and dense thorn thickets made the trail a twisting snake-track that often almost vanished in front of them. This was apparently the narrow waist of the Badlands which swept in a vast circle around the western and southern approaches to El Angelo. The river which Ben had ridden alongside from the north wound around the western edge of the depression, but apart from this there seemed to be no water whatever in the area.

Brows puckered a little in thought, he sat tall in the saddle, looking about him for the first signs of Andrew Faulds's ranch.

It seemed so unlikely that the other would have chosen such a spot for a cattle spread. With only the river to provide water, it needed only a dam to alter the course of it, and he would be utterly dependent on whoever owned the land further north.

This was still a lawless frontier; a dangerous spot for an unwary traveller. The hills that lifted to the south-west were rugged and bare except for a thin stretch of timber halfway up their steep slopes. They looked wild and inaccessible, sparsely inhabited except for those men on the run from the law who may have chosen these out-of-the-way places where they felt they were secure.

The trail diminished in width until it was almost a game run, the ground rising steadily until they suddenly topped a straight, high-backed ridge and Ben saw immediately below them, a fertile plain whose existence he would never have guessed at until he had come in sight of it. The sun was down as they approached the grasslands but there were still a few hours of clear daylight left and it promised to be a fine, serene night.

'This is Faulds's ranch,' Lander said, pointing. 'Not as big as the Triple C, but big enough to give Manvell a headache. He knows he can't put too much pressure on the small folk until he's busted Faulds and that ain't been so easy in the past. But with him laid up as he is, and only his daughter to run the place, Manvell is goin' to find it a little easier, unless you stick around to stop him.'

'Daughter?' Ben glanced around at the other. 'First time I knew Andrew had any kin.'

Lander's bushy brows went up a little, then he nodded. 'She's been back East for some years. He reckoned that this was no place for a girl after her Ma died. She came back a couple of months before he was shot. She's been doin' a good job, but it needs a man's hand around the place, specially when you're dealin' with a snake like Manvell.'

Ben pursed his lips a little in reflective thought. The trail

31

wound away through the tall grass, cut up the side of a low, humped hill, then went on through pleasant park-like country, with trees growing on either side of it, thinly-timbered, and richly-grassed, the ideal sort of country for a beef herd. He could see why Manvell had cast envious eyes on this stretch of territory. Far off to their right, the mountains curved away along the horizon in a wide sweep and the last rays of the sun were just touching their sky-reaching crests with a crimson glow, like the reflection from some vast fire behind the horizon.

A small herd of cattle grazed peacefully on the brow of the hill and Ben saw the small handful of men keeping guard over them. The night crew, circling the beasts, ready for trouble. Normally, it needed only a couple of men to keep an eye open for any strays, but now, in these troubled times, there were a dozen men close at hand, with just the one fire burning at their line camp near the timber.

'Ready for trouble,' he observed, nodding his head in their direction.

'You'll learn all about that when we get to the ranch,' said Lander tightly.

It was almost an hour later when they sighted the ranch buildings, in the bend of a small valley between the rising hills. It was an excellent spot for the ranch, close to a narrow stream, evidently a tributary of the river they had ridden by earlier, set at a point where the hills funnelled both wind and heavy rain away. They crossed a plank bridge, the hollow sound of their mounts' hoofbeats announcing their presence for the door of the ranch opened as they rode into the square courtyard and a girl appeared on the porch. She held a Winchester in her hands, pointed at them, but the gun was lowered as she recognized Lander.

She walked down into the dust, came forward. Ben glanced at her closely as she stepped forward towards them. Tall and slim, she wore a pair of faded levis and a checkered shirt, tucked into the broad leather belt. Her hair was a rich auburn that curled around her shoulders, glinting a little in the light. She's still young, thought Ben, and a little scared. Not used to the ways of the frontier yet, having been back East for so long and now she's been tossed in at the deep end, having to take over the responsibilities of running this spread. It was, he knew, a task that would have taxed anyone even if things had been quiet, but with a full-blown range war in the offing, if Manvell suddenly made his mind up to fight, it would be almost beyond her control. She drew herself erect, watching him a little suspiciously, still not quite sure of him even though he rode in with her foreman.

Lander said, stepping from the saddle, 'This here is Ben Littlejohn, Miss Alison. You've heard your Pa talk about him.'

Ben stepped forward as the girl lowered the rifle and held out her hand to him. 'I'm glad to meet you, Marshal. Dad often talks about you. He said you might be riding this way soon, though he didn't tell me how he was so sure.'

'He figured there might be trouble startin' soon,' Ben said easily, turning his mount over to Lander and falling into step with the girl. 'But I must confess I never knew he had a daughter and I thought I knew him quite well in the old days.'

The girl laughed a little and from the sound of it, Ben guessed that it had been some little while since she had laughed. 'He always said that this territory was no place for a woman until it had been cleaned up of the coyotes who inhabit it. I didn't know what he meant then, but since coming back here, I've found out only too well. There are evil men and evil ways here which we have to fight and eliminate before this country will ever be peaceful.'

Ben nodded. He went inside after her. He had not expected a girl to have had such an insight into the problems which the western frontier faced at that time. Evidently she knew the score. 'I reckon you're talkin' about Carrico

Manvell.'

Her face became suddenly serious. 'He's the worst of them all,' she said sombrely. 'He's brought in a band of killers and he aims at taking over everything and everybody. He's already done most of it by killing or intimidation. He owns most of El Angelo and several of the smaller ranches. He either killed or terrorised the men who owned them, forcing those who were still alive to sell at ridiculously low prices. Now he's got the biggest spread and the largest herd in the territory and he's getting bigger and more powerful every day.'

'You think he was the man who gave the order to have your father shot?'

'I'm sure of it. But I can't prove anything. Even if I could, there's no law and order here to make any charges stand against him, or to carry out any sentence. The circuit judge comes around once every three months and he does as Manvell says. So you can see, there's very little we can do.'

'Couldn't all of the small ranchers band together and finish this for good?'

She shook her head. 'Even with all of them in it together, we don't have as many men as he does. He's more than forty gunslingers on his payroll, almost all of them wanted killers from other parts of the territory.'

She paused outside one of the doors, then went on: 'Dad will tell you all you want to know. He's been waiting for you for some weeks now. I think he finally gave up all hope of you coming.' She paused for a moment with her hand on the knob of the door. 'Do you really think you can help as, Marshal?'

He smiled a little. 'The name is Ben – and I'll do everything I can to help. I've already had a run in with one of Manvell's men.'

He saw her eyes widen a shade. Then she pressed her lips firmly together, opened the door and said: 'Someone here to see you, Dad. An old friend of yours.'

Ben went inside the bedroom, glanced down at the man propped up to the iron bed set against the far wall. Andrew Faulds was naked from the waist up with a wide bandage around his chest and shoulder. He looked white under his usual ruddy tan and Ben saw, with a faint pang of surprise, the change which had taken place in the other since they had last met. He seemed to have aged in the seven years or so which had passed. The lines on his face were deeper and more numerous now. His right arm was thrown back over the bed, grasping the bedpost.

'I never figured we'd meet in circumstances like these, Andrew,' Ben said, going forward.

The other grinned, even above the pain of his hurt. Sweat was beading on his forehead and he wiped it away with his left hand. But there was a deep warmth to his smile as he said: 'Glad to see you, Ben. It's been a long time. I only wish we could have met under happier conditions.'

'I've heard a little of your troubles,' Ben said. He pulled forward a chair and sat down beside the other. 'Maybe if you were to tell me a little more.'

From the doorway, Alison said: 'I'll fix you something to eat, Ben. You'll be famished after that long ride from town.'

'Thanks.' He nodded, smiling. 'I'd sure appreciate that.'

When she had closed the door, Andrew Faulds said quietly: 'Things are gettin' real bad now, Ben. I thought, a little while ago, that I could control them, but now I'm not so sure. I've had to let Alison do most of the chores around here, runnin' the place, keepin' an eye on things. Lander has helped, but he's no gunfighter and I need a man who can handle a gun and stand up to the polecats who're tryin' to take this place from me.'

'Carrico Manvell.'

The other drew his brows together into a straight line. His jaw tightened. 'That's right, Ben. He's been bringin' in men for months now, ready for a showdown. Unless we can stop

35

him now, we're finished – and he knows it.'

'He had some of his men staked out, watchin' for me ridin' into town,' Ben said grimly. 'A gunslinger by the name of Ed Fazer called me in the saloon.'

'Fazer!' said Faulds in a gritty voice. 'His right hand killer. I knew there might be trouble, but I didn't figure they would know you were ridin' in. What happened to Fazer?'

'He's in the morgue right now,' Ben said tautly. 'He drew on me and I was forced to gun him down.'

'He's dead!' There was a momentary surprise in the other's tone. Then he nodded slowly in understanding. 'I might have known. You were always the fastest with a gun that I ever knew. Guess you're still as fast. Fazer was good. He's killed plenty of men who tried to stand up to Manvell. Maybe once he hears about this, Manvell may pause a little before makin' any fresh move. It's bound to upset his plans a little.' There was a fierce glint in his eyes now and his hand clenched tightly into a hard fist on the sheet.

'And what happened to you? I heard you were tryin' to stop some *hombres* from rustling off some of your herd.'

The other shifted on the bed, easing his weight from one side to the other. Silently, he gritted his teeth, struggling with the pain of his smashed shoulder.

'There was a big bunch of them. They hit us without warnin'. I saw Fazer ridin' with them, leadin' them in. We drove them off in the end, but not before two of my men were killed and I got this bullet in the side. Grazed across a rib and then up into the shoulder. Made a fine mess I can tell you. The Doc reckons I won't be able to use this arm properly for some months, even after the flesh has healed.'

He shrugged his shoulders and the movement brought a fresh stab of agony in the wound and he gasped with the pain of it, the sweat popping out afresh on his brow, teeth clenched tightly together.

'What happened to the last sheriff you had in town?' Ben

asked, after a few moments' silence.

'Cal Henders. Trouble with him, he was gettin' on in years. Weren't as fast with a gun as he used to be in his young days and he knew it. He turned a blind eye to Manvell's activities for a while, hopin' maybe that they wouldn't last, that the citizens would recognize him for what he was, a cheap, tinhorn gambler and run him out of town, saving him the trouble of goin' up against him. But it didn't turn out that way and when Manvell and his boys burned down the newspaper offices for printing some warning to the town against them, he stepped in and tried to bring Manvell in. Duprez, one of Carrico's hired gunmen shot him in the back one night while he was makin' his rounds of the town. Since there was nobody willin' to stand for the post, we've had no law here at all, unless it's Manvell's law.'

Ben nodded slowly. It was a picture which he had seen many times and in several different places. There would be a period of reasonable stability, enforced by a sheriff quick with a gun. Then there would be the old ways of violence creeping in, inflexible and unchanging, and the only law would be that of the sixgun. Invariably, it needed someone of iron will and a fearless disposition to bring things back to normal again.

Faulds bared his teeth and gripped the bedpost more tightly with his fingers. He said thinly: 'I don't suppose you would be willin' to stand for marshal in El Angelo, just for a while until we can put Manvell here he belongs?' He made a hopeful plea.

'What makes you think that the townsfolk would want me as marshal, even if I was willin'?' Ben asked. He felt a slight sense of surprise at the other's proposition. 'I reckon that they would know what it would mean, more violence and more bloodshed. It always happens that way before you get law and order again. Manvell won't concede defeat without a fight and unless I could get some backing from the ordinary folk in town, it would make that job well nigh impossible to carry out. Force the issue and Manvell is likely to ride in and burn the town.'

'At least it would force his hand and it might force the other citizens and the smaller ranchers to realize where their only hope of salvation lies.'

'I guess I'd like a chance to think about that,' Ben said. 'After all I do have a job and—'

'I understand that, Ben. But can't you see that you're needed here more than you are back in Denver. That town is orderly now that you've had a hand in cleanin' it up. We need somethin' like that here and I'm convinced that you're the man to do it. I know that I still have enough influence in town to get you that appointment as marshal in El Angelo.'

Ben hesitated. Inwardly, he could see the other's position; but he could also see the difficulties of such a move. Manvell would strike at once, before his position was seriously challenged. He could not afford to have anyone in town who would challenge his authority, particularly anyone who would refuse to knuckle down to him and carry out his orders. It was debatable, even if Andrew was able to talk the Town Council members into appointing him marshal there, if he could get together any men who would stand with him against the hired gunmen that Manvell could send into town to shoot up the place. Still, it was something to which he would give his attention.

He was spared the necessity of giving an immediate answer by Alison. Opening the door, she said quietly: 'I've got the meal ready for you, Ben. I'm sure you can talk to Father later. Right now, it's more important that you get some hot food inside you.'

'Thanks, I certainly appreciate that.' Ben got to his feet, scraping back his chair. Glancing down at the man on the bed, he said: 'Well, Andrew, we'll talk about this later.'

'Consider what I've said, Ben. It could be the makin' or the breakin' of this town.'

Ben nodded, followed the girl into the kitchen at the rear

38

of the house, where the meal was laid out for him; sweet pota-
toes, peas, fried meat, hot coffee on the stove. Seating himself
at the table, he realized for the first time just how famished
he really was. The girl sat opposite him and watched as he ate,
devouring the well-cooked food ravenously. She did not
speak until he had finished and the plate was clean. Then, as
he sat back and built himself a smoke, with his second cup of
steaming coffee in front of him, she said seriously:

'What do you think we should do, Ben? Stay here and try
to fight Manvell, or sell out while we have the chance and
we're both still alive? They showed the last time that they
mean business. Dad is lucky to be alive right now. The next
time he may not be so fortunate.'

'Your father is a stubborn man, especially when he believes
in what he's fighting for, and at the moment, he does. The
fact that Manvell has tried to kill him has only made him
more determined to stay and fight. He never was a man for
running away from trouble and I figure he's too old to start
now.'

'Is he really so stubborn?' she asked. She placed her hands
around the cup of coffee and stared down at it miserably.

Ben hesitated, then nodded. 'I knew him in the old days,
Alison. I rode with him, taking every different trail we could
find. They were good times we had then. But there came the
parting of the trails. He wanted to settle down, build himself
something permanent, a ranch where he could work out the
rest of his days. As for me, well, I guess I was the restless kind.
I had to keep on riding, finding out where one trail led, then
starting on another one, following it to the end. I was in
Denver when I got his letter asking me to come as quickly as
I could, warning me there was big trouble brewing here.'

'And you came running,' said the girl softly. 'You didn't
have to come. This was a deal of his making.'

'Your father saved my life once. I owed him this favour.
There was also the tie of all the days we'd spent together in

the past. Things like that aren't easily forgotten.'

'I think I can understand,' said the girl warmly. She sipped her coffee slowly, eyeing him over the brim of the cup. 'And now that you're here, what do you intend to do?'

'I don't know. Your father wants me to run as marshal of the town. He thinks that he can get the Town Committee to offer me the job.'

'Perhaps he can. From what I've heard, they'd offer it to anyone who would accept it.'

'Even if Manvell went against it?'

Her eyes gave him an appraising glance. 'You certainly have a point there, Ben.' She watched him with a moment's narrowing attention, her gaze curiously penetrating. 'For you, of course, that doesn't really matter, does it?'

'About what Manvell thinks?' He paused, then shook his head. 'Not for myself – no. But as far as the safety of the town and anyone in it is concerned, I'd have to consider such an offer very carefully.'

'I think you ought to take it,' said the girl promptly. He had the feeling that her words were prompted more by impulse than clear thinking. When she went on, he felt sure of it. 'This town has brought many of its troubles on itself by not backing up the sheriff we had when Manvell first arrived here. If they had, it would have been possible to have run him out of town before he became as powerful as he is now. They really deserve all they get, if it has to be done to bring law and order back.'

'I gather that you don't think much of the Town Committee.'

'I don't.' Her voice sharpened just a little. 'They're like a bunch of scared jack-rabbits, afraid to do anything for fear of Carrico Manvell.'

'Perhaps you shouldn't blame them too much. In my time, I've seen towns that have been hit by range-riders. It wasn't a nice thing to see. These men have the lives of the ordinary citizens to think about.'

Alison Faulds studied him over a thoughtful interval. 'I wonder what really goes on in your head, Ben,' she said softly. 'You may be right about the Town Committee. If this were happening back East, there would be some sort of law on Manvell's trail. But this is open, empty country and it seems to be a matter of indifference whether men are shot or cattle rustled. This is how the big outfits got started in the first place, taking beef from the others and having enough men to hold the cattle once they got them onto their range. That's how it will go on until somebody big enough steps in and calls a halt to it all.'

'And you figure I may be the one to do it?' There was a faint trace of amusement in his tone and he saw instantly that she did not like it.

Her eyes flashed as she said: 'Of course, if you don't like the idea of stepping up against these killers . . . .'

'I didn't say that. But I always like to know what I'm ridin' into before I make any decisions. It pays for a man to be real cautious when dealin' with snakes like Carrico Manvell.'

Alison let out a long sigh. The stiffness which had come to her face, the look of cold containment, slipped. She was tired and showed it and it was clear that depression was chilling her spirit a little, even though she had not wanted him to know it. She struggled inwardly with her thoughts, then pushed back her chair, got to her feet and said: 'I'll clear the things away. If you want to talk with Dad again, he'll still be awake.'

'I reckon I'll just take a quick look around.' He moved to the door, stepped out into the cool air, stood for a moment on the porch building a smoke, then walked across the courtyard, the spurs raking up tiny eddies of dust behind him. He leaned against the wooden rails of the corral, watching the horses, then glanced up towards the low hills, dark against the sky.

As he stood there, he tried to think things out in his mind

in the light of what he now knew. He had already decided that, if Andrew could swing things with the Town Committee, he would take the job of marshal here. He did not like the idea of leaving Manvell with enough time in which to make his plans and put them into operation. If he could force the other's hand, Carrico might make a mistake. A man who was being pushed into things, sometimes acted without thinking of the possible consequences of his actions.

Drawing the smoke down into his lungs, he listened to the various night sounds around him, the mournful lowing of the small herd of cattle high on the slope of the distant hill, the nervous movements of the horses in the nearby corral. He let the smoke out through his nostrils. The facts had to be faced, he thought grimly. As far as he could see, Manvell held all of the cards here. He had the men, the guns, to back his play. The killing of his right hand man, Ed Fazer, would provide him with an added incentive for wanting to kill him. Whatever it was he had started here, first by riding into El Angelo in answer to Andrew's letter and secondly by shooting it out with Fazer, he knew for certain that it would not be an easy thing to finish.

He decided that, apart from letting Andrew talk the Town Committee into appointing him Town Marshal, he ought to wait for Manvell to make his next move.

THREE

TOWN MARSHAL

The day was hot and oppressive with a faint muttering of thunder in the far distance beyond the desert. The flies had been troublesome and seated in his office, Carrico Manvell felt disinclined to exert himself any more than was absolutely necessary. The growing heat made him feel more irritable than usual and when the door was thrust unceremoniously open and Hank Calleen came in without knocking, it was the last straw as far as he was concerned.

Manvell felt enraged but he showed no sign of it other than by the sudden narrowing of his eyes and a tightening of his lips as he looked Calleen over. 'What the hell do you mean by bustin' in here like that?' he demanded harshly.

'Trouble brewin', boss,' said the other jerkily. 'I figured you ought to know about it right away.'

'What kind of trouble?' asked the other warily.

'That *hombre*, Littlejohn. Faulds sent word into town asking the Committee to meet and approve Littlejohn as Town Marshal, says it's about time El Angelo had some real law and order.'

Manvell sat taut in his chair for a moment, face set and fixed. Then he allowed himself to relax, dug into his vest pocket and brought out a thin black cigar, thrust it between

43

his lips and lit it, blowing the smoke out in front of him. Finally, he said, his voice very soft: 'So that's the reason he wanted Littlejohn here. I'm beginnin' to see things now.'

'He ain't like the usual sheep we have to deal with,' Calleen said carefully. 'He knows how to use a gun and if he should get the townsfolk on his side and willin' to back his play, it could mean the end for us. I guess there ain't anythin' we can do but kill him before he starts any trouble.'

'I'll decide whether he's to be killed or not,' Manvell said thinly. He furrowed his brow in sudden thought. 'I guess that Faulds wouldn't put Littlejohn up for Town Marshal if he didn't figure he had a chance of takin' the folk here with him. Maybe he wants us to make a try at killin' Littlejohn.'

'You're really playin' with fire if you let him take over the town,' Calleen pointed out.

'He'll be killed,' said Manvell, 'but in the right place and time.' He shook his head slowly, as if talking to a child. 'I can't seem to make you understand that we have to be cautious in this. I've got most of the folk in town really buffaloed right now, but I've seen similar cases where sheep have suddenly turned into wolves and even I don't have the men to go up against the whole town if they did turn and back Littlejohn. A man has to be cautious and clever, or he doesn't last long. Don't worry, I'll get the job done.'

'Then you won't try to stop 'em if they do elect him Town Marshal?'

Manvell grinned viciously. 'Why should I? If he takes on that job, there are far more chances for us to see that he's shot down, than if he hides out at Faulds' place and only comes out of hidin' when he's watchin' for us rustlin' the beef off the range. I prefer to know exactly where he is most of the time. That way, he'll leave me free to take care of the other chore I've got in mind.'

Calleen eyed the other in perplexity for a long moment, then went out. Manvell heard his footsteps fading into the distance along the hollow-sounding boardwalk. He drew on the cigar, staring into the sunlight that slanted down through the dust-motes in the air. The news had shaken him a little.

It was not quite what he had expected. But now that he came to think about it, there was no doubting the logic behind it all.

Reaching behind him, he poured himself a drink. He was nursing a very odd feeling and the drink did not help as he had hoped. This mood, this irritation, the unsatisfied, curiously formless feeling, would not leave him. Sitting loose in his joints, he pondered over the problems which this recent news had brought to him. Then he took a second drink and finally a third before getting to his feet and putting the bottle back in the cupboard behind the desk.

There had been no word from Mentor concerning old Charlie Monroe. Either the old coot was still up there in the mountains someplace, maybe looking for that gold and silver even now, or he had somehow slipped past Mentor and was in town. If he was questioned by Littlejohn before he could get to him, then things might be black. The thought brought a rising urgency into his mind, one which he could not throw off. The fox in his brain kept at him, telling him that there might be very little time. Once he got his hands on that treasure, he would no longer have to worry about the ranch or rustling stock from the other ranchers. He would have more wealth than he knew what to do with, could ride on to some place where the law would never find him, change his name, and live in luxury. That gold and silver plate would buy anything that a man could wish for.

Ben Littlejohn walked through the lobby of the small hotel, went up to the man who sat sprawled in the wicker chair at the far end near one of the tall potted plants. The other stirred and opened one eye, then jerked himself up sharply as he saw who it was.

'You'll be lookin' for the rest of the Town Committee, Marshal, I guess,' he said, getting to his feet. He pointed a finger towards one of the doors. 'They're in there, waitin' for you.' He smiled faintly. 'I can't say I'd be sorry to see you installed as marshal here. Manvell has been lordin' it over the town for too long now. But I do know that it's goin' to bring trouble here if you do take on the job.'

'Because I don't aim to back down in the face of everythin' that Manvell says?'

'That's right. You don't look to me to be the sort of man who's likely to back away in the face of threats no matter who makes 'em.'

'Stick with that impression,' Ben told him. He moved to the door, knocked and then opened it, going inside, and closing it behind him. There were five men seated around the long oaken table in the room. He recognized one or two of them from previous meetings with them. Bellamy, the banker, gave him a brief nod, motioned him towards the empty chair at the other end of the table.

'Please sit down, Marshal.' he said courteously.

Ben lowered his loose-limbed frame into the chair, let his glance move over the faces around him. Sol Grainger, Hepper, and two men he did not know.

Bellamy introduced them, nodding in their direction. 'I don't reckon that you've met Forbes and Conder, the other two members of the Committee,' he said. 'We've been discussing this letter we received from Faulds. You must know of the ah – difficulties – associated with the post of Town Marshal.'

'Concerning Carrico Manvell, you mean.'

'Yes. He's a big man in this part of the territory, holds quite a lot of stock in the bank and naturally one must consult his wishes in any matter which concerns the running of the town's affairs.'

'Meanin' that if he said no – then you'd have to follow his orders?'

'Not exactly. You misunderstand our position here. If we were to elect you as Town Marshal, it could be either a good thing or a bad thing for the town and that's the one thing which is our concern. Most of us have wives and families to think of. Manvell could fire this town, shoot up the place, any time he chose and if you figure that one man, no matter how good he was, could stand against the crew of gunslingers he could bring in, then you're being a fool.'

Ben kept his temper with an effort. He could see these men's point of view, even though he knew that it was a narrow one and the wrong one in the end. A town never succeeded in bringing about law and order without some sacrifices and the longer it put off facing the facts, however distasteful they might be, the worse it became.

'Then just how long will you allow things to go on as they are? I've seen this happen before, not once, but many times, I've even helped to clean up towns when they've been dominated by men as ruthless as Manvell. It ain't easy, I know. But it has to be done sooner or later. Ain't no sense puttin' it off until Manvell can get so big that there's no chance at all of stoppin' him.'

Bellamy nodded. 'We looked at it that way and then put it to the vote. It came out four to one in favour of offering you the job, if you want it.' His lips tightened a shade. 'I don't intend to tell you the identity of the man who voted against it.'

'Does Manvell know about this?'

Bellamy's lips were set hard against his teeth. 'I reckon he will by now. He has eyes and ears everywhere in town.'

There was a moment of uneasy silence in the room. Ben guessed that one or two of these men were regretting their decision already, but he gave them no opportunity of changing their mind. Rising to his feet, he said quietly: 'Desperate cases need desperate remedies, gentlemen. Some of the things that I may have to do you won't like, but if this town is to have any semblance of law and order, then you'll have to put up with them.'

'Now don't go shootin' off at any old tangent,' warned Conder harshly. He looked dubiously at Ben. 'I've heard of your reputation and I know that you're a good, honest man, and fast with a gun. But when you start buckin' Carrico Manvell, then you'll find that you have a real coyote by the tail and that could be bad, not only for you, but for the rest of us. When he's killed you, then he'll take it out of the town for hirin' you in the first place. Better take things easy for just a while until you get used to the feel of a place like El Angelo. You may discover that it's a mite different from those other towns you've known in the past.'

'I'll bear that in mind,' Ben said tersely. 'But I'm acceptin' this badge on one condition. That if it does happen to come to a showdown I can call on the citizens of El Angelo to back me. A marshal is no use at all unless he has the town behind him in what he has to do.'

'Well now, that's going to depend on what you mean to try,' said Hepper cautiously. 'I for one don't aim on getting into too much trouble with Carrico until I see how things are going. He's a pretty rough customer and—'

'It's either that or you can stay here and stew in your own juice,' Ben told him. 'And I figure you can guess what that may mean. Once he finds that he can do as he likes in town, he'll ride roughshod over every one of you. He'll take over El Angelo and grind it into the dust and none of you will be able to stop him. My way, at least you'll have a chance.'

'What sort of a chance?' inquired Bellamy. There was no fear in his tone, Ben noticed; only a sort of mild curiosity.

Ben shrugged his shoulders. 'I reckon we'd better wait and see what Manvell decides to do when he hears of this. I'd have figured he'd have made some sort of move against Andrew

Faulds before now. Somethin' must be forcin' him to hold his hand and I sure wish I knew what it is.'

The night chill had dissipated quickly once the bright sun had risen and there was a flat, breathless heat lying over the ridge that slanted down the side of the mountain. The man rode out of the trees and coarse scrub and checking his mount on a low rise of ground which looked down on to the flat land stretching east towards the river, he sat forward a little in the saddle. The years had smoothed and pared the flesh on his bones and his hair was as white as the mantle of snow which at most times covered the crests of the tall mountains, but he still sat ramrod straight in the saddle as he had in the old days when he had ridden with the men who had gone south into Mexico during the Border Wars.

His name was Charlie Monroe, born in the town called Memphis some sixty-eight years before, moved west with one of the first wagon trains to leave for California, stopped off somewhere along the Texas border, acted as scout for a unit of Sibley's force during the invasion of 1862, fighting beside George Bascom when the captain was killed at Valverde on the Rio Grande, prospected for silver along the border with New Mexico for close on fifteen years, and finally finished in the little town of El Angelo close to the border, within ten miles of the Rio Grande.

The narrow stage road which tumbled over the ledge and into the wide crack in the earth, crossed the bridge a couple of miles further on and then swung right into a small side gorge to begin its final twelve miles of tortuous twisting and winding towards the town on the edge of the Flats. He waited for a few moments, listening to all of the sounds about him, then rolled and lighted a quirley, pushed his hat further back on his head and narrowed his gaze against the sun, watching the horse and rider far out on the trail, so distant that they were cut down to the size of a slow, snail-moving dot.

Sitting there, he speculated on the rider in the distance. He might be a cowhand from one of the small ranches along this stretch of territory for there were a few who ran their cattle in the lower reaches of the hills, out of the way of men like Carrico Manvell; but Monroe thought he knew most of the men by sight and he had seen this man ride by early that morning, had watched him from the straggling brush where he had made cold camp during the night. He looked a tough one, there was no doubting that, with his gun hung low on his hip and judging from the coat of white dust which had lain on man and horse, the other had been riding the hills a long way since resting up.

Flicking the butt of his smoke into the dry earth, he gigged his mount and started along the low ridge beside the tall cedars. Spiny crests tipped up on both sides of him as he entered the long, sprawling canyon and here and there, long streaks of red sandstone broke through the cedars and showed up starkly against the brown and green of vegetation and earth.

He thought about that other man as he rode, his mount picking its way slowly and cautiously through the upthrusting boulders, shying away at times wherever a purple sand lizard skittered from one sun-baked rock to another at their approach. Whoever the other was, he had not been born and raised in mountain country. He moved too hard, made too much noise, seemed to spend more of his time fighting the country than riding with it, letting it lead him around the rocky curves and corners as a mountain man would do. The other's mount would be fair tuckered out by the time he had angled down to the plains fronting the town. Charlie had spent so many years in the mountains and hills that he was a part of them, knew virtually every trail there was in this range, every hideout used by the men on the run from the law. He was on nodding acquaintance with most of these men who, for the most part, held no interference with him, regarding him as a crazy-headed old fool who spent his time looking for gold dust where none had ever existed, seeking some long-lost Eldorado where he would strike it rich and move back East to spend the rest of his days in peace and luxury.

He grinned a little to himself, swaying easily in the saddle, thinking of that small scrap of paper which reposed in his shirt pocket, neatly folded, well-thumbed now. Someday, when he felt the urge again, he would go off and look for that treasure and maybe this time he would find it. He tried to recall how long ago it was since he had made his initial attempt to locate it. More than seven years before, he reckoned, although his mind kept getting kind of hazy whenever he tried to remember dates and years. But that sandstorm had blown up from the north-east while he had been out in the alkali and had forced him to give up the attempt for the time being. He figured it was now more than eleven years since he had come across that dying man in the desert. He had tended him for close on a week before he had finally died of the gunshot wound which had burned right through his lung and shoulder. The other had been Spanish, he reckoned, and he had understood very little of the lingo, but had picked up enough from the man's ramblings towards the end to understand that the treasure of San Miguel which had been taken from the monastery and buried in the hills not many miles from El Angelo, had its whereabouts marked on the map which the other had pressed into his hands shortly before he had died.

It was an hour after noon when Monroe rode out on to the long, sloping incline which led down from the foothills in the direction of the plains. He had followed the other rider's trail until it had suddenly veered from the main track and headed up into the rocky ridges that crowded down above him, in places actually overhanging the trail. For a moment, he had debated whether or not to swing off and follow the man, then had decided against it. So long as he knew where he was, he felt certain he would be able to keep an eye on him.

*

Swinging down from the pines, Mentor swept a wary glance along the narrow trail that wound and twisted its way beneath him. He had reached his vantage point just after the sun had climbed to its zenith. Now he dismounted, pulled his horse back among the rocks and went forward until he reached a spot from where he could see the trail for almost a quarter of a mile in either direction. He had picked up Monroe's trail the previous day, had checked the spot where he had made camp, circling carefully around it to make sure that it was the right man. Now he felt reasonably sure that the other was somewhere behind him, making his way forward along the main trail. Some time that afternoon, he would be forced to pass this point and when he did, he meant to be ready for him.

During the night, when he had been scouring the hills for Monroe, he had made up his mind what he intended to do once he caught up with the old fellow. One thing was for sure. He wouldn't wait for Monroe to ride on into town, and then light back to the Triple C to warn Manvell of his arrival. That way, he would see none of the gold himself.

He thinned his lips back over his teeth as he rested the barrel of the Winchester in a V formed by two slant-sided slabs of rock, and waited, feeling the heat of the sun burn down on the back of his neck and shoulders. He pushed his hat further back on his head in an attempt to shade his neck, sweat beading his forehead and beginning a slow trickle down his face and into his eyes. Once he had killed Monroe and had that map in his possession, he would ride on out of this stretch of the territory, up into the hills. With the gold in his saddle-bags he would head south, over the frontier, where Manvell would never find him. He had made his plans and he felt sure that his chances of succeeding were good. Had he figured it otherwise he would never have dared to go up

52

against Carrico in this fashion.

The minutes began to drag. Still there was no sign of Monroe on the trail. He watched the point where the trail came out of the timber a quarter of a mile to his left. Here, he was protected from a chance view by anyone higher in the country above him and that was how he wanted it. Anyhow, who was there to see him? The men who lived in these wild and virtually inaccessible places cared little for what went on around them so long as it did not represent a menace to them and Monroe was the only other man he had spotted along the trail since he had been watching it for nigh on a week. But the uneasy feeling persisted in his mind. A man could get the fidgets real bad in this country if he kept imagining unfriendly eyes watching him from every rock and bush. Once, he lifted his head and remained tautly in that position for almost two full minutes, every nerve and muscle strained, listening and studying the land around him for fear that there might be danger to him rather than to Monroe. Except for the rustling wind in the thorn thickets and the slither of a copperhead as it moved sluggishly through the brush in the day's heat, there was nothing and the afternoon was deathly quiet.

He needed a drink of whiskey to put fire into him, he decided thirstily. It was several days now since he had a drink. Manvell would be back there in town living it up while he waited it out here, carrying out orders; and he would get nothing out of it in the end unless he went through with the plans he had formulated during the past day or so.

Though the sun had moved a little from its zenith, it was still a white, glaring disc of fire high above him, throwing few shadows, giving no shade and in spite of his hat, it felt as though his skull was slowly being fried. He took in a long, gasping breath, felt it burn like fire in his chest. His lungs seemed unable to extract sufficient oxygen for their needs. Where the hell was Monroe? Why hadn't he shown up before now? He couldn't have been less than half an hour behind him during the morning. Maybe he had stopped alongside the trail for a bite to eat, but even that should not have kept him so long.

Sweat trickled into his eyes and he rubbed it away angrily with the back of his hand. The glare, refracting from the rocks on all sides of him, was a sickening brightness that made it difficult for him to make out the finer details of the trail below him. He had slept little during the past two nights and the strain was beginning to tell on him now. His head drooped forward onto his arms, eyes lidding and closing.

The sudden sound in the near distance jerked him wide awake, hands reaching out automatically and closing around the Winchester. He squinted into the vicious sunglare, searching for the source of the sound. The sand had clogged his mouth and nostrils, making every breath a rasping torture and his grip on the rifle tightened as he saw the faint movement among the trees where the trail emerged from the timberline. His lips thinned back over his teeth. Lifting the rifle carefully, he sighted on the spot, waiting for Monroe to ride out into the open. One shot ought to be enough at that distance, he told himself. Then to get the map for himself and head up into the hills after the treasure. He could scarcely contain himself and in spite of the tight grip he had forced on his emotions, his hands trembled violently on the rifle. Savagely, he pushed his sight through the shimmering curtain of heat and light which threatened to blind him. He had to make sure with the first shot. Old as he was, Monroe was known to be pretty handy with a rifle. A man did not live all these years on the frontier without becoming adept at shooting fast and straight when the necessity arose.

The movement at the edge of the timber stopped. Leaning forward a little, Mentor squinted through narrowly-slitted eyes, trying to make out just where the other was. He thought he saw the momentary flash of sunlight off the metal pieces of a bridle, but he could not be sure and he did not want to risk a shot for fear of warning the other. He was forced to wait, feeling the tension grow in him, a slow, climbing sensation that convulsed the muscles of his arms and legs, knotting them in painful spasms of cramp. Blinking his eyes rapidly to dispel the dragging weariness that threatened to overcome him, he checked the bullets in his rifle, then waited with a sharp tenseness.

Still the other did not move out into the open. It was almost as if he knew that Mentor was there waiting to bushwhack him. A hoof turned on rock and the sound brought Mentor sharply upright into his knees. The sound had been behind him, not at the edge of the timber. The crashing echo of the gunshot, hammering off the rocky walls of the stone chimney at his back reverberated in his ears a split second after he felt the leaden impact of the slug in his left shoulder. Pain burned its way along his arm and down into his back and he cursed solidly as he rolled swiftly into cover, ducking his head instinctively as he waited for more bullets to head in his direction. Snickering back the hammer of his rifle, he steadied it, gritting his teeth as the sharp spasms of agony lanced through his body. Whatever happened, he must not panic. The other was up there, among the rocks that overhung his hiding place. The damned old fool must have spotted his tracks, guessed what lay in store for him and climbed higher than he was, waiting until he could see him directly before risking a snap shot. His only chance, he knew, was to get to his horse and ride out while the other was still crouched down among the boulders. He did not doubt his chances of outrunning Charlie Monroe, wounded as he was. But first he had to get to his horse and that was not going to be easy. Lying flat on his chest as he was now, he was protected from the other, but the instant he showed himself in an attempt to get to the horse, he would be picked off like a wood pigeon. Monroe had shown only a few seconds before that there was nothing wrong with his aim.

Rolling over onto his side, he squinted up into the looming boulders, hoping to catch a glimpse of the other. For a long moment, the seconds dragged themselves into a sun-hazed eternity. The stillness was oppressive, like a blanket stretched over the scent. How he could have been such a goddarned fool to allow himself to be ambushed by the other, he did not know. There was absolutely no chance now of getting hold of that map unless he could outshoot the other; and in the present circumstances, he doubted that very much. His one chance was to get away with a whole skin. A gun flash split the sunlight and he swung his rifle sharply, loosed off a couple of shots in the direction of the muzzle flash, heard the slugs scream off rock and ricochet into the distance without hitting his target.

Ejecting the spent shell, he levered a fresh cartridge into the breech, sucking in a sharp intake of air as pain raced through him at the movement.

Slugs whacked leadenly into the rocks on either side of him and as he saw no sign of Monroe's head he guessed that the other was firing through a V in the rocks, was able to see his hiding place without lifting his head and exposing himself to return fire.

He fired another shot, then crawled forward over the rough ground, gritting his teeth tightly to suppress a moan of pain. It was a slow crawl. Every second he expected to feel the smashing impact of another slug in his body, this time in the heart or through the head. But none came. Very cautiously, he raised his head, stared through the shimmering heat haze to where his mount stood only five feet away, waiting patiently, the reins dangling towards the ground. But the ground was open here and he lay quite still thinking out his next move. It would not be long before Monroe guessed what he meant to do and shifted his position so that he could pin him down. More rifle fire came from the boulders above him, but this time, he wisely held his fire. Monroe was deliberately shooting down at him, trying to draw his fire and make him give away his position.

With an effort that cost him dear, he got his legs under him, waited tensely for a moment until he guessed that the other was having to reload, then thrust thimself forward, throwing his body across the intervening space which separated him from his mount. He had dropped his Winchester. Now he clawed for the dangling reins, caught them up in his fingers and levered himself to his feet. Pain burned through him as he was forced to drag himself up into the saddle. Sweat trickled into his eyes, half blinding him. But he hung on grimly, knowing with a sick certainty that if he once lost his hold, it would mean the end of him. Once Monroe saw him clearly, he would not miss with his next shot.

The horse shied away nervously as he swung up into the saddle, straightening his legs to keep his balance. Swinging, he jerked his Colt from its holster and sent a flurry of shots into the rocks as he spurred his mount away. Behind him, the gun flashes showed briefly and he heard the shrill whine of lead as it burned away from the side of the trail in murderous ricochet. The bullets had come perilously close and he urged his horse into a sharp run that was dangerously fast on the uneven ground and with his arm in its present condition. But he knew that he had to risk a fall if he was to get out of range of Monroe.

For several moments, he continued to turn his head every few seconds, straining to pick out the sound of any pursuit. Not until he had rounded a sharp bend in the trail and was half a mile from the spot where Monroe had ambushed him, was he fairly certain that the other had decided not to try to catch him.

Presently, as he rode through the lower reaches of the foothills, the going became easier and he made better time, still forced to cling tightly to the reins, gripping the horse's flanks with his knees, to stay upright in the saddle as weakness, brought about by the boiling heat and the loss of blood from the deep wound in his shoulder, threatened to overwhelm him. There was a throbbing ache at the back of his eyes that grew worse as the minutes passed and the sun glare was still sufficient to hurt his eyes.

Early evening found him riding along the bank of the river, less than a mile from town. By now, the pain in his shoulder had subsided to a dull, diffuse ache that was somehow worse than the initial stabbing agony. He rode the horse up to the river bank, slid weakly from the saddle and walked forward until the cool water came up to his knees. Then he bent and tried to wash the blood from his shoulder. It had congealed into his shirt and the cotton was sticking to the torn flesh so that he was forced to pull it away before he could wash it clean. The touch of the cold water stung his shoulder but he persisted, binding it as well as he could with a strip torn from his shirt. After his mount had drunk, he climbed back into the saddle, paused to stare along the shadowed trail behind him. He saw nothing of Monroe, although he guessed that the other was there somewhere, making his way more slowly and cautiously into town.

Distance and the growing darkness were his allies now. He knew that Charlie Monroe would not dare to try to follow him into town and force a showdown. He felt the slow anger in him. Not that it would make much difference if he did because this time, in spite of his shoulder, he would be ready for him and he would not miss. He knew he had to get the doc to take a look at his shoulder as soon as he could and he forced a brisker pace from his mount than before.

It was dark by the time he rode into the main street of El Angelo, headed towards Manvell's office close to the bank. He guessed that the other would be there at that time of the evening, unless he was in one of the saloons. As soon as he saw the yellow glow of lamplight in the window, he knew he had guessed right.

Looping the reins over the hitching rail outside the office, he was on the point of going inside when a dark shadow detached itself from the boardwalk in front of the building and moved out into the faint light from the window.

'Looks to me as if you've run into trouble, Mentor,' said Ben Littlejohn softly. He stood with his legs braced, his thumbs hooked just inside his belt, forward of the twin Colts at his waist.

Mentor stopped instantly, stared up at the other for a moment, mouth working but no sound coming out. The marshal was the last person he wanted to see at that moment. Stammering a little, he said harshly, 'Got shot at by some goddamned dry-gulcher, Marshal, back along the trail a piece.'

'You got any idea who it might have been?' There was no expression in the other's soft tone.

'None. Never saw him. He must've been lyin' in wait for me in the rocks overlookin' the trail. First thing I knew was when the slug hit me in the shoulder. I took a couple of shots at him, but I doubt if I hit him. I was too busy gettin' out of there to bother much about who he was.'

'You want to make any complaint? I could take out a posse of men and have a look around the spot if you care to tell me just where it happened.'

'That ain't necessary, Marshal. He'll be well clear of the territory by now once he knows he didn't kill me. Ain't no sense in you botherin'.'

'Suit yourself,' murmured the other. He stepped back into the shadows, then swung about, moved off along the dully-echoing boardwalk.

Mentor pursed his lips tightly together, waited until the sound of the other's footsteps had died away into the night stillness, then stepped up onto the slatted woodwork, rapped loudly on the door of the office. It opened a few moments later and Manvell stared out at him, paused for a moment, then stood on one side, motioning him in.

Mentor stood blinking against the light for a moment, noticed the other's eyes narrow in quick appraisal as he saw the rough bandage over his shoulder.

Roughly, Manvell said: 'What in hell happened to you?'

'I ran into Monroe along the trail. He jumped me, got in a lucky shot before I managed to ride on.'

'I thought I told you just to watch for him, not to try to kill him for yourself.'

'Now hold on there, boss,' said Mentor plaintively. 'I had him watched when he made camp, then trailed him. Somehow, he must've guessed I was behind him, because the first thing I knew he'd aimed this rifle shot at me from the rocks.'

'How do you know it was Monroe who shot at you?'

'I saw him duck back into the rocks as I loosed off a couple of shots at him. It was Monroe all right and he's headed for town.'

Manvell hesitated for a moment, then walked back around the edge of the highly-polished desk, stood behind it for a moment staring down at the papers on the top. Then he lifted his head and there was a snake-like glitter in his eyes as he faced the other man down. 'After this blunder, we'll be lucky if he rides into town. He'll probably start puttin' two and two together and wonderin' why you were tailin' him like that. If he was close enough for you to recognize him, he will have recognized you.'

'Ain't no real reason why that ought to have scared him off,' protested the other dully. He felt ill at ease with Manvell when he was in this mood. Inwardly he wondered if the other was also trying to think things out and whether he would figure that there might be something more to this than just a case of dry-gulching.

'I'll be the judge of that,' snapped Manvell. He opened the drawer of his desk, but made no move to take anything out, did not even look down at it.

'You want me for anythin' else, boss?' Mentor asked. 'This shoulder of mine is givin' me hell. I'd like to get the doc to fix it up for me.'

'Somehow, I don't think you'll be needin' the doc to fix that bullet wound. You've given yourself away, Mentor.' Something in Manvell's tone brought the other's head up with a quick jerk. Manvell had reached down into the open drawer in front of him. Now he pulled up his right hand and Mentor saw that there was a small, snub-nosed Derringer in it, pointed straight at his chest.

'What is this?' he muttered. 'If I made a mistake, then I'm sorry but—'

Slowly, Carrico Manvell shook his head. There was a thin smile on his pale lips. 'It was no mistake you made,' he said softly, very soft. 'The only mistake you made was underestimatin' Charlie Monroe. You figured it would be the easiest thing in the world to bushwhack the old coot, shoot him down from cover and then grab off that map for yourself. You meant to double-cross me, get that treasure for yourself and ride on out of the territory. Only Charlie had you figured right from the start. He was ready for you when you made your move. Soon as you found that you didn't stand a chance shootin' it out with him, you high-tailed it back into town, hopin' I'd be stupid enough not to see through your little plan.'

'Now that ain't so,' said Mentor harshly. He held out both of his hands in front of him as though trying desperately to ward off something evil. 'You know that I wouldn't double-cross you.'

Manvell raised his brows a fraction. The smile on his lips broadened for a moment and his knuckles grew white as he began to exert pressure on the trigger of the gun.

'I know that you won't ever try to double-cross me again,' he said tightly.

Mentor read the promise of death in the other's eyes. He knew that he had no chance at all, but instinct made him try for his own gun, his right hand striking down for the Colt. His fingers closed around the smooth butt, were in the act of drawing it clear of leather, when the bullet from the Derringer struck him in the chest, high up, pitching him drunkenly onto his knees, the Colt sliding back into its holster as he fell forward, his head striking the front of the heavy desk with a sickening thud.

FOUR

DEATH OF A HOBO

Sundown came and went before Charlie Monroe rode into town, taking his mount along to the livery stable and putting it in the back. When he emerged into the street again, feeling the cool wind that blew down off the tops of the distant mountains against his face, he stood for a moment with his shoulders against a wooden upright, building himself a smoke. He stood there, bent forward slightly, a grey indistinct figure and remained that way until he had the cigarette in his mouth and lit.

His thoughts kept him busy and uncertainty gnawed continually at his mind. Why had that *hombre* tried to bushwhack him along the trail? Some killer who had heard of that scrap of paper he carried, wanting to find out for himself if the rumours he had heard were true, maybe go out looking for the treasure himself. Or had it been something more than that? He pondered over it. For the first time in many years, he felt uneasy at riding into town. Every shadow now seemed to hold a menace, every movement was a gun being laid on him. With an effort, he shrugged the feeling away. A man could imagine all sorts of things if he got to thinking like this, allowing his thoughts to run away with him.

Stepping down into the dust of the street, he made his way

out to the edge of town. The light from the windows threw his face alternately into light and shadow and his eyes moved swiftly from side to side, watchful for trouble.

Outside Felipe's Eating House, he paused, swept a quick look up and down the street, then pushed the door open with the flat of his hand and went inside. Felipe was seated in his usual place behind the desk at the end of the small lobby. His glance lifted as Charlie went in, then he grinned warmly, his teeth showing white in the shadow of his face.

'You have any luck in the hills this trip, Charlie?' he asked, taking down a key from the wall at his back.

'Just a little, Felipe.' Monroe took the key, hefted the small sack on to his back. 'Enough to pay for a few drinks and a bed for a few nights.'

'You know you're always welcome here, Charlie,' nodded the other. 'The usual room at the top of the stairs.'

Monroe moved across the small lobby and climbed the creaking stairs to the upper floor. Very few men ever came to this place now. In the old days, when he had first come to El Angelo, and there had been plenty of prospectors such as himself, scouring the hills, panning for gold and silver in the swift-running streams, Felipe had done a roaring trade. Now it was just the drifters and saddle bums who put up here for the night on their way through, some running for the border, others seeking work on one of the ranches.

Unlocking the door of the room, he stepped inside, closed the door and locked it, then felt his way forward in the darkness. The window was a square of faint light giving little illumination by which to see. His knee caught the edge of the iron bed and he cursed softly under his breath, fumbled in his pocket for matches, struck one and found the lamp on the small table. He lit it carefully, placed the glass chimney back on, then straightened, half-turned.

Instinct warned him of danger a split second before the voice behind him said: 'Hold it right there, Charlie. Don't make any funny move for that gun or it'll be the last move you make.'

Monroe stopped the downward swing of his right hand, turned very slowly. His face showed his surprise and feelings as he said sharply through his teeth: 'What do you want here, Manvell?'

The gunman shrugged. The Colt in his right hand was lined up on the older man's chest and his finger was bar-straight on the trigger. 'They tell me that you carry a map around with you, Monroe.' Manvell got to his feet as he spoke and moved forward, jabbing the muzzle of the gun hard into the other's midriff. Charlie gave a grunt of pain and stepped away until he felt the side of the table in his back and could retreat no further. There was a wolfish grin on Manvell's features.

'I don't carry a map with me,' Monroe said truculently. 'A map of what?'

'You know damned well what I'm talkin' about, you old fool. Now quit stallin' and hand it over. Otherwise, it's goin' to be the worse for you. I don't want to have to kill you, but I will if I have to.'

'You gone plumb loco, Manvell?' Charlie asked. His beard stuck out in defiance at the other. 'You bust into my room and start askin' fool questions about a map and—' He broke off with a gasp of agony as the foresight of the other's Colt suddenly raked across the side of his face drawing blood from his cheek. Manvell's smile was not pleasant now.

'You're just wastin' my time, Monroe,' he said thinly. 'If you want to die for your principles, that's all right by me. I've given you the chance to hand over the map of the San Miguel treasure peaceably.'

'That one of the varmints who rides for you tried to kill me along the trail?' Charlie asked tersely.

Manvell nodded. 'He was a goddamned fool. He won't make the same mistake again. My guess is he was tryin' to get that map for himself. He's dead now, as you will be in ten seconds if you don't find some sense.'

He cocked back the hammer of the gun with an ominous click that sounded loud in the stillness of the room, watching the sudden look of anticipatory fear that sprang into the other's eyes, noticing the way the other's tongue flicked out, wetting his lips nervously. This was the kind of situation that Manvell always found highly interesting; following the other man's frightened reactions. He drew unhurriedly on his smoke as he watched Monroe put up a hand and run a finger tremblingly down his cheek. He wagged the revolver in his hand.

'I'm waitin', Monroe,' he said silkily.

'All right, damn you, Manvell,' snarled the other. He dug into his shirt, pulled out the piece of paper and tossed it down onto the table. Manvell's eyes lit up greedily. His lips thinned back over his teeth as he sucked in a sharp breath of air, gusting it down into his lungs.

'Now you're showin' sense,' he said hoarsely. He stepped back a pace, kept the gun pointed at the other, ready for any tricks, then reached out with his left hand and snatched up the map, glanced at it quickly out of the corner of his eye before stuffing it into his own pocket.

'You'll never get your hands on that treasure, Manvell,' said Monroe from deep in his throat. 'I'll follow you every goddamned step of the way and sooner or later, I'll catch you without a gun in your hand or with your back turned.'

'I'll never give you that opportunity,' Manvell said. 'I've got enough men in town tonight to ensure that you stay here. If you want to play it tough, then I'm sure they'll be able to accommodate you.' Manvell spoke tightly, but his concentration was all on the map in his pocket. He did not doubt that it was the genuine article and his mind was already filled with a sense of heightened anticipation. His mind was working ahead to what he would find once he followed the directions given on that scrap of paper and he was already counting the money he could get for the gold across the border.

Across from him, Monroe began to tremble a little, not from fear now but from a feeling of delayed anger that somehow managed to overflow the fear. 'You dirty thievin' bastard, Manvell,' he gritted. 'You murdered that gunhawk of yours just to make sure that he wouldn't get a share of it.'

Manvell's eyes glared with the fire of greed too much to withhold. 'Never you mind what I did or didn't do, Monroe. You ain't goin' to have long to worry about it.'

Monroe guessed the meaning behind the other's words as Manvell swung up the gun slightly. He dived instinctively for the man's right hand, but missed his clutch. The next instant Manvell struck him savagely at the side of the head with the barrel of the gun, sending him staggering to his knees. Desperately, Monroe caught Manvell around the knees, tried to hang on while his senses returned.

But his opponent kicked him savagely in the ribs, sending him sprawling. The next moment, he levelled the gun on the man who lay at his feet and pulled the trigger once. The weapon jerked against his wrist and he saw Monroe twitch as the slug bit deeply into his back, knocking him flat onto the floor.

Slowly, the ringing echoes of the shot died away. Manvell stood quite still for a long moment, staring down at the dead man lying on the floor, then he moved towards the door, hesitated as he heard the sound of footsteps running up the stairs and moving cautiously along the corridor outside, halting near the door. There came a hesitant rapping of knuckles on the door.

'You all right in there, Charlie?'

It was Felipe's voice. Manvell moved over to the window, glanced out into the darkness of the street, There was a balcony running along the wall just outside the window. Easing the window up gently, he clambered out onto it, felt the cold night air sweep around him for a moment. Shivering, he climbed along the balcony, made his way to one of the other windows and prised it open, stepping into the dark room beyond. He had taken a calculated risk that the room would be empty; but judging from the number of folk Felipe had staying at this place, he knew the chances were in his favour.

The door was open and stepping out into the corridor, he caught a glimpse of Felipe standing outside the door at the far end, twisting the handle. It was dark and shadowed in the passage and he tiptoed softly along to the stairs, moved swiftly down them, out through the narrow lobby and into the street.

Ben Littlejohn angled his way through the deep dust of the street towards the small eating house at the edge of town. Stopping on the boardwalk in the shadows cast by the faint beam of light shining through two of the windows, he pushed his hat higher onto the back of his head, silently cursed the whims of fate which seemed to delight in making things happen in the middle of the night when all decent citizens were supposed to be asleep.

The message that there had been a killing in the eating house had reached him at the office five minutes before, the man who had brought it shaking him awake with urgent hands. As if there had not been enough trouble, what with the shooting of Mentor, Manvell's right hand man since Ed Fazer had died, trying to outdraw him on his first day in town. There were still several unexplained features about that killing which were nagging at Ben's mind, but he put them all from him as he went inside.

The Mexican who met him at the bottom of the stairs had a worried look on his dark features. He said excitedly: 'I heard the shot, Marshal. It come from inside Charlie Monroe's room. I called out if there was anything wrong, but got no answer, so I busted the door in.'

'And you found Charlie Monroe dead?'

'*Sí.*'

'Reckon you'd better show me where he is,' Ben said tautly.

He followed the other up the stairs, along the passage at the top and into the room at the far end. The old, grey-haired man lay huddled on the floor just inside the door. Bending, Ben turned him over, noticed the stain on the back of his dusty jacket where the slug had hit him between the shoulder blades from close range. He guessed that the other had died instantly.

Getting to his feet, he said: 'You got any idea who might want to kill him like this?'

Felipe shrugged. 'He had no enemies that I ever heard of, Marshal. He came into town now and then and always stopped with me. He knew he was welcome here at any time, whether he could pay for lodging or not.'

'Did he have any money this time?'

'He said that he had had enough gold for a few days in town.'

Ben went through the old man's pockets, found the small bag of dust and opened the leather thongs. It was almost full of the dully gleaming powder which had been panned from the streams high in the hills.

'Strange that whoever did this, didn't go through his pockets and take this,' he observed. 'Must have been that the killer just wanted him dead, or there was somethin' more important than gold that he was after.'

There was a movement just inside the doorway and Bert Thompson, one of the town deputies came in. He eyed the body on the floor with a cursory glance, then said to Ben: 'Heard what you said there, Marshal. What could be more important than gold?'

'That's what I ain't got figured out yet,' Ben said softly. He scratched at the stubble on his chin. 'But there's just a glimmerin' beginning to show. You heard that Mentor rode into town with a gunshot in his shoulder?'

Thompson nodded. 'You reckon that's got somethin' to do with Charlie here?'

'Could be. If Mentor was watchin' the trail, lookin' out for Charlie ridin' into town, knowin' that he had something valuable on him, he might try to dry-gulch him, hopin' to get his hands on it, whatever it was. But not knowin' Monroe he'd not figure that he could read trail better than most and might turn the tables on him. I figure that Carrico Manvell is at the back of this. He'd send Mentor out to watch the trail, but if Mentor tried to double-cross him and grab off for himself whatever it was that Monroe was carryin', then it would explain why Mentor was killed this evenin'.'

'And Carrico killed Charlie here?'

'It makes sense,' Ben allowed.

'You'll need proof of that before you can make a move against Carrico,' warned Thompson.

'I know. I reckon there are a lot of folk in this town who would like to see Carrico Manvell brought to justice, but they're all shakin' so much in their boots that they'd never back any move I made, proof or not.'

'You think he could have been after the map that Charlie carried?' asked Felipe, from the doorway.

'That was nothin' more than rumour,' Thompson said.

'Maybe and maybe not,' Ben murmured. 'I've heard of this map he's supposed to have had, showing where that treasure from the monastery of San Miguel is hidden some place in the hills. These maps are a dime a dozen, but there's just the chance that this one is genuine. If it is, then I can well imagine Manvell killing for it.' He hitched his gunbelt a little higher around his waist. 'Guess I'll pay a call on Mister Manvell.'

Thompson lifted his brows in mild surprise. 'You goin' to see him tonight?'

'Can you think of any better time?' Ben asked pointedly. 'If he did have anythin' to do with this killin', then he'll still be in town and not out at the ranch. I know for a fact he was here a couple of hours ago. There was a light on in his office shortly before Mentor rode in and the fact that his body was found in the alley not far from Manvell's office, is another pointer in the right direction.'

'Want me to come along with you, Marshal?'

Ben shook his head. 'What I have to say to Carrico Manvell will be short and to the point,' he said tersely.

Ben left the eating house, made his way slowly and purposefully along the street. There were still plenty of men around even at that time of night, he noticed, some of them undoubtedly Manvell's men, roaming the town just in case any trouble broke. There was the feel of trouble abroad in town that night. Whether the two killings had brought it on or not, he wasn't sure. But he could feel that little itch just between his shoulder blades and he knew that it would pay him to tread warily until he was sure of his ground.

There was still a yellow light burning in Manvell's office. Rapping loudly on the door, he waited for a moment, then thrust it open and went inside. Manvell was bending in front of the safe set against the far wall. He whirled and came upright in a single movement as Ben walked in, his right hand streaking for the gun at his hip. Then he stopped his hand and forced himself to relax as he saw who it was standing there.

'Why, Marshal,' he said, smiling half-heartedly. 'What brings you here at this time of night?'

'Just want to ask you a few questions, Manvell,' he said evenly. 'Reckon you know there's been another killin' in town tonight.'

Manvell said smoothly: 'Heard a shot a little while ago. Seemed to come from the edge of town. Figured it was nothin' more than a high-spirited cowpoke loosing off some steam.'

71

'Then you figured wrong. Somebody sneaked into Charlie Monroe's room and shot him down in cold blood.'

'Now why would anybody want to kill Charlie?' Manvell said harshly. He locked the safe, came back and slumped into the chair behind the desk. Pulling out a bottle, he poured himself a drink, gestured with the bottle, then smiled faintly as Ben shook his head. He tossed the drink back, grimaced faintly as the raw liquor hit the back of his throat. 'Far as I know, he had no enemies in the world. He was nothin' more than a harmless old fool who wondered into town occasionally, then vanished again. He had some place up in the hills where he'd made a gold strike a while back. Nothin' big, you understand, but enough to get him some dust so that he could come into town once in a while and go out on a drinkin' spree. Nothin' wrong in that, I guess.'

'Funny though that one of your men should ride into town with a slug in his shoulder a couple of hours before Charlie Monroe gets here, ridin' in from the same direction. Odder still that Mentor gets himself shot in that alley close by here and then Charlie gets his a little later.'

Manvell's eyes narrowed a little. His voice was tight and thinned as he said: 'You tryin' to say that there's a connection between these events, Marshal?' He poured another drink, splashing the whiskey into his glass, spilling a little on the top of the desk. 'Don't rightly see how there can be.'

'No?' Ben levelled his gaze on the other. 'I searched Charlie's body back there in the eating house. There was a small bag of dust in one of his pockets.'

'So? What does that prove?' For a moment the colour had entirely gone from the other's countenance and the insolence and pride in his own confidence seemed to have vanished. Even so – there was something left, a stubborn belief in himself that made him meet Ben's gaze with a dead, empty stare.

'It proves that whoever killed Charlie Monroe did so either

because he had some feud against him – or because Charlie
had something on him that was more valuable than a bag of
gold dust.'

'Such as?'

'The map showing the whereabouts of the San Miguel
treasure.' Ben watched the rancher's face closely for any reac-
tion to this remark. He was not entirely disappointed. He saw
a faint spot of colour burn high in Manvell's cheeks and a
sudden startled look come into his eyes.

With an effort, Manvell forced a quick bark of a laugh, sat
back in his chair and tried to appear at ease. 'So you've heard
these stupid rumours too, Marshal. The stories of the treasure
of San Miguel are many and none of them can be believed.
There is no such map, unless it's a forgery. And how would a
man such as Charlie Monroe get his hands on it even if it did
exist? He's been an out-and-out saddlebum all his days,
panning for gold in the hills and then ridin' into town to get
roarin' drunk once in a while. If he had a map such as you're
talkin' about, why didn't he go after this fabulous treasure?'

'Maybe he did – once,' Ben said quietly. 'But if he wasn't
lucky enough to find it then, it could be that he never made
another attempt.'

'So what do you get from all this?' the other's tone had
hardened and he let his gaze rest for a moment on the guns
slung low at the Marshal's waist.

'You're the man who gives the orders around here when
it comes to keepin' a watch on the trails. My guess is that you
ordered Mentor to watch for Monroe ridin' in. When you
figured that Mentor had double-crossed you, tryin' to kill
Charlie and get the map for himself, you killed him,
dumped his body in the alley where it wouldn't be directly
connected with you, then went out to the eating house and
waited for Charlie to show up. After killin' him, you took the
map.'

Manvell released a deep breath. He shook his head very

slowly. 'That may be an idea you have, Marshal. But you can't prove it.'

'Might be that I can in time,' Ben told him. 'In the meantime, I don't want you to leave town until I've investigated these killings a little further.'

Manvell's lip curled into a thin sneer. 'How do you aim to stop me, Marshal?' he asked. 'With that gun of yours and the three deputies you've got? They ain't enough and you know it.'

'I've got a gun here that says you stay in town until I tell you that you can leave,' Ben said grimly. 'I'm the law in this town now and anybody who tries to step out of line has to answer to me.'

Manvell lurched heavily to his feet. His face was flushed now, both from anger and the whiskey he had consumed. Leaning forward over the desk, resting his weight on his arms, he said thickly: 'I guess we'd better get this straight right here and now, Marshal. Sure, you got yourself elected marshal of El Angelo, but you know damned well that if I'd let it be known I didn't want you there, the citizens of the Town Committee would never have appointed you.'

'All right,' said Ben softly, 'I realize that and I figured it was odd at the time. So why did you string along with them?'

'Because you didn't worry me in the least and you still don't. You're just a fast man with a gun, a man who's been lucky in the past. But there's a limit to the luck a man has and I can finish you any time I like. You reckon I don't know how you've been tryin' to talk the other ranchers into bandin' together and goin' up against the Triple C? I knew that the night after you started. But you won't get them to follow you. Even if they joined forces, they would only muster half as many men as I've got at my call; and my men are seasoned gunfighters. Better think that over before you do anythin' foolish, Marshal.'

Ben stared at the other levelly, his face expressionless.

Then he shrugged his shoulders. 'You're buckin' the wrong man this time, Manvell. Maybe I've got no real proof right now that you killed Mentor and Charlie Monroe, but I sure will have and when I do, I won't come talkin', I'll come with a gun and a rope to put around your neck. It'll be a real pleasure to see you danglin' from the nearest tree.'

'Try that, Littlejohn, and see just how far you get. Maybe you're wearin' a badge right now, but that means nothin'. I'm the real law here and my say-so is enough. Now let me give you a piece of advice. The last sheriff we had here tried to step out of line. He finished up in the dust with a slug in him. The same thing could happen to you quite easily.'

Ben grinned down at the other and there was something cold and menacing in the mirthless smile that the other moved back a little. 'It's been tried before, Manvell. Nobody's succeeded yet.'

Turning on his heel, he moved to the door, turned as he reached it. The other was still standing behind the desk, his body leaning forward, face etched in shadow by the yellow lamplight.

Ben said easily, with deadly calm. 'I'll stand you under a hanging tree, Manvell, if I find that you killed Charlie Monroe. As for Mentor, I feel no concern for him. He was just another gunslick. But Charlie meant no trouble to anybody.'

He closed the door before Manvell could make any reply, walked along the narrow alley where Mentor's body had been found earlier, then through the streets which were quiet now, circling the town twice before he was finally satisfied, going back to the sheriff's office. El Angelo was silent now and he seated himself in the chair behind the desk, resting his legs on top, leaning back with his hands clasped in front of him. It was not an easy position in which to get any rest, but he had slept in more uncomfortable postures before.

The next morning, Ben was wakened by a rough hand on his shoulder. He opened his eyes to see Lander standing over him. Getting to his feet, he said: 'What's on your mind, Lander? Somethin' happened at the ranch?'

'We got hit again last night. A bunch of the Triple C riders tried to haze off some of the herd. We drove 'em off but two of our men were killed.'

'You get any of them?'

'One *hombre*. Nicked him in the arm and shot his horse from under him. He's at the ranch now.'

'You reckon he can be made to talk? If he does, we could pin these rustlings on Manvell and that would be enough proof to hold him in jail until the circuit judge comes around,' Ben's mind was working fast, thinking ahead. This might be the lucky break he had been hoping for, an excuse for getting Manvell behind bars where he could hold him until he had a chance to probe a little further into the two recent killings. Manvell would deny that he had had any part in the rustling, of course, but when confronted by one of his own men he would have a difficult task trying to talk himself out of it.

'I'll ride out with you and question this *hombre* myself,' he said. 'Just as soon as I've had a bite to eat and given Thompson his instructions to keep an eye on Manvell.'

'They tell me there was some shootin' in town last night,' said the other as he followed Ben to the door, then along the street to the small restaurant.

'That's right. One of Manvell's gunhawks and Charlie Monroe got it. I'm pretty certain that it was Carrico Manvell himself who pulled the trigger both times, but as yet I haven't been able to prove it.'

'Why should he want to gun down Charlie Monroe – unless it was for that map he carried.'

'Then you've heard about it too.' Ben lowered himself into the chair at the table, signalled to the Chinese cook, who brought hot coffee over and then a couple of plates, piled high with bacon, two eggs, beans and bread.

'I've heard that he had this map. Never seen it,' nodded the other. 'But it was common knowledge that he carried it around with him. You figure it was the real thing?'

'Maybe. Manvell seems to think so.'

They finished the rest of their breakfast in silence, then went back to the sheriff's office. Thompson was already there when they arrived.

'I'm ridin' out to Andrew Faulds's place,' Ben told him. 'There was a gunfight there last night after a bunch of *hombres* tried to rustle some of the cattle. I reckon I should be back shortly after noon. Keep an eye on Manvell while I'm gone. He may try to get his riders together and force a showdown.' He did not mention to the other any details of the talk he had had with Manvell the previous night, or the order he had given the rancher to stay in town. There was just the chance that Thompson might try to stop Carrico if he made a move and none of the deputies, although they were all good men, would stand a chance in a shootout with any of Manvell's men – or Manvell himself for that matter.

Picking out his mount from the livery stable, he rode beside Lander along the dusty street, aware of the curious eyes that followed them. He knew that there had been some talk in town that he had already thrown in his lot with Andrew Faulds and that he was therefore prejudiced and not open-minded as a marshal ought to be.

But that was something he did not intend to face until this was over and he had the proof against Manvell that he needed. What the rancher had said to him the previous night still rankled in him, mostly because however much he hated to admit it, he was forced to recognize its truth. Manvell did have the gunmen in town and at the Triple C ranch to back up any play he cared to make. Even if the other ranchers and the townsfolk got together, it was doubtful if they could stop him. For a second, he stared down at the badge pinned on his shirt and a grim bitterness welled up into his mouth, wrinkling his features in a grimace. It did not really stand for very much until he had put Manvell in jail and brought him to trial for murder. Even then he would have to fight for justice, since the circuit judge might be on Manvell's payroll.

The sun lifted from the horizon, began its invisible path across the sky; the heat had risen too, sunlight glaring at them from the rough, craggy ground that lay on either side of the trail until they finally rode over the low range of hills, taking the narrow, winding trail that led down to the ranch-house.

Alison Faulds met them at the door. Her face looked troubled, but she managed a brave smile for Ben as he swung down from the saddle and advanced towards her.

'Lander will put your horse into the corrall,' she said. 'Come inside, Ben.'

'I hear you had more trouble last night, Alison,' Ben said, when they were seated in the small parlour. 'Where's this *hombre* who was shot?'

'A couple of the boys are keeping watch on him, Ben.' She twisted her fingers a little nervously in her lap, then looked up. 'When is all this going to end? Do we have to sit here and wait for Manvell to wear us down, to steal all of our beef and kill all of our men. They shot two in last night's raid. There's no telling how many more will die the next time. Sooner or later, he's going to realize that he'll have to send in a larger force of men. When he does, it could mean that we're finished.'

'I only wish I could say that he won't come at you again, Alison. But I can't do that. He's still determined to smash you and he'll do it by any means in his power. I think, myself, that there's a showdown comin' very soon. There were two killings in town last night. One of Manvell's men and an old prospector called Charlie Monroe.'

He saw the look of distress on the girl's face. 'Charlie Monroe.' There was a note of incredulity in her tone. 'But why would anyone want to kill him?'

78

'I've got the glimmerings of an idea, but no real proof. Soon as I get that, I'm goin' after Manvell. I'll shoot him down if I have to. Reckon it might be best if it comes to that anyway. If he comes before the circuit judge, chances are he'll get away with it.'

'Then there's nothing you can do at all?'

'Not exactly. If I can get this gunslick to talk, I can at least arrest Manvell on a charge of being connected with the rustlin'. It may not hold him for long, but perhaps long enough for me to snoop around a little more.'

'He's a crafty man. Besides, he has plenty of friends and gunhawks riding with him. What's to stop them marching on the jail and breaking him out?'

'Nothing, I guess. Only it would give me a chance to shoot 'em legal that way and also show the townsfolk of El Angelo the sort of man they're dealin' with. It's goin' to need somethin' like this to shock them out of their fear of him. Once they rise and turn against him, he's finished for sure.'

'It will mean that a lot of innocent people will be hurt and killed.'

'I know,' Ben nodded his head slowly, soberly. 'But when it comes to a showdown like this, innocent people are always hurt. If only they stood up to violence and corruption in the beginning when it is easier, then they wouldn't have to face a showdown now. But they always try to take the easy way out, and like gophers, they hide their heads in the dirt and pretend that if they don't look, everything will fade away.'

'I hope that you know what it is you're starting. Manvell won't give in easily.'

Ben smiled faintly, rubbed the side of his jaw. 'More than likely you're right, Alison. But let's have a word with this man you captured. Could be that he'll tell me a few things I want to know.'

'I think you'll find he's very stubborn,' said the girl. She rose to her feet, led the way outside, to a small hut at the rear of the ranch-house. There was a man standing outside, a rifle in the crook of his arm. He dropped the butt of his cigarette into the dirt and ground it out with his heel as they approached, straightened up a little.

'Clem is inside, Miss Alison,' he said, opening the door. They stepped through. The Triple C rider was stretched out on a rough bed in one corner, while Clem was seated in a high-backed chair, his rifle over his knees. He grinned broadly as he saw Ben.

'Here's your man, Marshal,' he said, but the grim tone belied any mirth in his smile. 'One of that murderin' crew that shot down Slim and Beckett. If it wasn't that you might have liked a talk with him, I was all for stringin' him up from the cottonwood yonder.' He jerked a thumb towards the huge tree which grew on the edge of the courtyard.

'Don't worry, he'll hang for rustlin'.' Ben said tightly. He stood beside the bed and stared down at the man lying there. He did not recognize the other, but he looked the usual type of man who rode with big outfits like the Triple C.

'You workin' for Manvell?' he asked harshly.

The other opened both eyes and stared up at him, then twisted back his lips in a sneer. 'I've got nothin' to say to you, lawman,' he grunted.

'There are always ways of makin' you talk, my friend,' Ben said. His tone was quite expressionless, but there was something at the back of his eyes which made the other pause, then prop himself up on the bed on his good shoulder.

'Carrico Manvell won't stand for this once he hears about it. He'll come ridin' with the rest of the boys and take this place apart, piece by piece, and string up everyone here.'

'That doesn't make your position any better,' Ben reminded him. 'You might be interested to know that I learned a lot of old Indian tricks during the years I spent along the frontier, all of them guaranteed to loosen stubborn tongues like yours.'

80

The other's confidence was beginning to slip and for the first time he did not seem to be so sure of himself. Whiningly, he said: 'You've got to get me to a doctor with this shoulder of mine.'

'I'll get that tended to as soon as you talk.' Bending, Ben caught hold of the other's arm, tightening the hold of his fingers just below the elbow. He saw the beads of sweat come out on the man's forehead as he continued to apply pressure. 'Now – are you goin' to talk? Who gave the orders that you were to ride against this ranch? Was it Carrico Manvell?'

'I'm not sayin' anythin',' said the other through clenched teeth. He squirmed sharply on the bed, trying to roll away from Ben, but the other slowly pressed back on the man's arm, bringing it hard against the joint so that agony jarred redly through the limb.

'You still goin' to be stubborn?'

The other gasped, the breath whistling through his teeth. His legs threshed vainly as he strove to pull away. Ben knew that Clem and the girl were watching him, but he also knew he had no other choice now that he had committed himself. If he got this man into town to a doctor before questioning him, Manvell would doubtless send men either to get him away from Ben, or to kill him so that he would be unable to talk.

Deliberately, Ben twisted the other's arm, saw the stain on the bandage grow as the movement opened the wound afresh. The muscles of the man's jaw lumped under the stubbled skin and his eyes widened in shock and pain.

'All right, all right, I'll talk,' he said thickly. 'Just stop twistin' my arm.'

Ben relaxed the pressure a little, but still retained his grip. He had the impression that the other would speak the truth so long as he forced it out of him by this means. 'Then talk!' he snapped harshly. 'You're workin' for Carrico Manvell?'

'Yeah. I ride for the Triple C,' grunted the other. 'For

81

God's sake be careful with my arm. I—'

'Who gave the orders for you to ride against this place and haze off part of the herd?'

'Manvell. He gives all the orders on the Triple C.'

'Better be sure of that. Because you may have to testify about it when we bring Manvell in for trial. And just in case you're thinkin' of backin' down when it comes to the point, these folk here will act as my witnesses and I'll shoot you down the minute you start lyin'.'

He released his grip on the other's arm, stepped back. 'Now get on your feet and don't try any tricks. I'm just itchin' for a chance to kill you.'

The other hesitated for a moment, staring up at Ben with an expression of utter hatred written on his snarling features. Then he swung his legs slowly to the floor and staggered upright, clutching at his injured shoulder. His lips were twisted into a grimace of pain as he stumbled towards the door with Ben and Clem moving close behind him.

Outside, the man leaning against the wall said: 'You want any help to take this critter into town, Marshal?'

Ben shook his head. 'You've got a job to do here, boys. Those *hombres* may strike again, though I doubt it after the maulin' they got last night. But in case they do, be ready for 'em. Perhaps you'll see more action here than in town.'

FIVE

SIX-GUN TRAIL

It was almost the height of day and the heat was fierce with the sun blazing down from a cloudless sky, when Ben Littlejohn rode into El Angelo with his prisoner. He kept his eyes on the boardwalks as he moved his mount along the whitedusted street, noticed the way in which curious eyes watched them, noticing who his prisoner was. He caught the faint murmur of voices from the street corners, saw two men, lounging in the shadows, suddenly jerk themselves upright and move off quickly, angling towards Carrico Manvell's place.

Well, the other would get to know sometime. It was impossible to keep news like this secret in a town the size of El Angelo and if there was to be any trouble, the sooner he got wind of it, the better.

Reining up in front of the jailhouse, he motioned the rustler from his saddle, slid the gun from its holster and jabbed it into the man's ribs, urging him onto the boardwalk and into the office. There was nobody there when he entered and this puzzled him for several moments. He had expected one of the deputies to be there, waiting for him to get back. Thompson ought to have warned one to be on duty until he returned. Maybe whoever it was had stepped across to the

83

canteen for a bite to eat, he decided.

'All right,' he said tightly, 'through that door there and no funny moves.'

The gunhawk shrugged, moved towards the door leading to the cells at the back of the building. He said through his teeth. 'Like I warned you, Littlejohn, you won't be holdin' me long. Carrico will have me out of this jail before sundown and when he does, I'll be comin' after you with a gun in my hand.'

'Any time you care to step up against me, you're welcome,' Ben gritted. 'Only it will be the last move you make.'

Unlocking the door of one of the cells, he pushed the other into it, slammed the door and locked it again. The man said grittily: 'You goin' to get the doc to take a look at this shoulder of mine?'

'I'll do that when I have the time,' Ben said. 'Now just make yourself at home.' He turned to make his way back along the passage, then paused at a sudden sound from one of the other cells. Swiftly, he moved back, to the very end of the passage, peered in through the bars. There was a shadowy figure lying on the low bunk in the cell, and as he watched, the other rolled over, then sat up, clutching at his head. It was Thompson.

Swiftly, Ben unlocked the door, went inside as the other tried to get to his feet. 'What happened, man?' he asked tersely. 'Who did this?'

The other shook his head groggily. He winced as Ben's fingers touched the side of his scalp gently. There was an ugly discolouration there where he had evidently been hit hard with some weapon, possibly the butt of a revolver.

'It was Carrico Manvell, wasn't it?'

The other nodded, sucked in his breath sharply as pain lanced through his skull. 'He came askin' for you. I said you were over at Faulds's place and he said he'd probably see you some other time. I never figured out that he might be up to somethin'. I thought he'd gone out again and I was just

84

moving to the door when he sneaked up on me from behind. That's the last I know until I came to in here. Where is Manvell now? I'd like to get him at the end of a gun. I'd—'

'Just try not to exert yourself,' Ben took the other's arm, led him out of the cell. 'I guess I know where Manvell is right now.'

'You know. Then where is he?'

'Out on the hill trail somewhere, spurrin' his mount as fast as it will go. He's got Monroe's map and he's headed for that treasure.'

'You mean to go after him?'

Ben nodded his head and answered grimly: 'I sure am. I figure he's either alone or he's taken only one of his boys with him. He won't want too many lookin' for that gold and silver. Not if he means to take most of it for himself.'

'What do you want me to do, Marshal?'

'Better get the doc to take a look at that head of yours. Then bring in a couple of deputies and keep a watch on that *hombre* in the other cell. He was one of the bunch rustlin' Andrew Faulds's cattle last night. There may be an attempt to bust him out of jail.'

'Sure thing,' Thompson nodded. 'I'll fix that right away, Ben.' He touched the wound on his head. 'Sure you don't want anybody to ride with you? That Carrico is a mean customer.'

'I'll find him,' Ben said grimly. 'This may be the chance I've been waitin' for. If I can nail him out there, I reckon that the rest of the wild bunch who ride for him will fold up. They're like sheep. They need somebody to lead them, to give the orders for killin'. Without that, they'll drift.'

'Hell, I sure hope you're right. But watch your step with Manvell. He's a killer and as fast with his gun as any of his men. He wouldn't have got to be where he is now if he wasn't.'

Carrico Manvell rode through the narrow cut of a dry creek,

sheltered from the sight of anyone on the main trail by the steep-sided banks of weathered sandstone that glowed redly in the light of the late afternoon sun. Now that the final quest for the San Miguel treasure had begun, he could feel the heightening tension rising in his mind, blotting out every other emotion. He wanted to talk yet as he glanced out of the corner of his eye at Jeb Saunders riding alongside him, he knew that there was little point in talking to the other at the present time. He had chosen Saunders to ride with him on this trail because he was the fastest man with a gun in his outfit and he did not doubt that Littlejohn would try to trail him once he rode back into El Angelo and found Thompson locked inside the cell. Maybe he ought to have finished the other while he had been about it, he thought viciously. Dead men told no tales. Yet he felt sure that it would not have taken long for Littlejohn to put two and two together even if he had killed Thompson. It might have made the marshal more eager to follow him than at present.

Saunders was a short, broad man with black hair, unkempt, that hung in strands beneath his broad-brimmed hat. His features were heavy and the deep-set dark eyes lacked intelligence. He was, however, a cunning, dangerous man, deadly with a gun and his fists and what he lacked in intelligence, he made up for in an unexpected speed, agility and strength. It had been said that Saunders was always in an angry, killer mood, but whenever Manvell had been around, he had succeeded in keeping it tightly under control, so well in fact that little sign of emotion ever escaped him.

The bed of the creek, made up of cracked mud baked hard from long exposure to the blistering heat of the sun, wound and twisted along the shadowed grave-like course of the stream long since gone. They approached the end of the run and Manvell spoke for the first time in almost fifteen minutes: 'Keep quiet now, Saunders, and keep your eyes open for trouble.'

'You reckon he'll come after us?'

'I'm sure of it. He'll know where we're headed and he won't waste any time. It'll be up to us to spot him first.' The way he said it made it clear to the other what they would do when Littlejohn did catch up with them and Saunders nodded his bull-like head in approval.

Gradually, the steep walls of the cut lowered and they rode out into more open country again, with the first of the timber still some miles distant. They had paused several times during the early afternoon to check their directions from the rough map, but now Manvell felt reasonably certain he knew the way they had to travel and where they ought to hit the treeline. Besides, they had wasted enough time already trying to decipher the old map. Many of the letters were faded now with the years and the writing was all in Spanish which he only understood slightly. Still, he figured he could understand enough to get him to the spot where the treasure taken from the San Miguel monastery was buried.

Those old monks had known how to hide their loot, he thought greedily. They had not taken it a mile or so from the monastery which was, he knew, close to the frontier with Mexico. They had brought it many miles up north of the border where it was less likely that the gringos would find it. He drew his lips back in a vicious grin. Too bad that they had not lived to get the chance to dig it up again and take it back to where it had come from originally. But their bad luck had been his good fortune.

He no longer doubted the authenticity of the map now. Even though that old fool Monroe had been carrying it around in his vest pocket for God alone knew how many years without heading out to get it for himself, he felt sure there had been some reason why the other had not got it and headed across the border with if. Maybe he'd tried before now and failed to find it. Maybe it meant very little to a man like him. He had always maintained that Monroe was a little touched in the head. No man in his right mind would carry anything worth as much as this for all that time, without making a try for the stuff.

They angled their mounts up into the rocks, again, eyes scanning the dusky overtones as the lowering sun threw longer and darker shadows over parts of the trail. Every few minutes, Manvell would turn in the saddle and stare behind him, slitting his eyes against the red sunglare, on the look out for the tell-tale smudge of smoke behind them which would tell him that Littlejohn was there, trailing them. He turned things over in his mind, deliberating whether the lawman would bring anyone along with him. He wasn't sure how Littlejohn would react once he heard that he had defied him and left town. Caution told him that the other was not a man to take chances and he would bring together a small posse to back him up. But the more he thought about it, the more he felt sure that Littlejohn would pursue them alone. There was more to this than just making sure he did not get his hands on the gold and silver. This had now become a personal thing between Littlejohn and himself and because of this, if nothing else, the other would ride after him alone. He would doubtless bank on the fact that a solitary rider could sneak up on his quarry with more chance of success than a bunch of men.

There was a twisting continuation of the cut a hundred yards away on their left, angling steeply downward. Saunders pointed to it, said harshly: 'Why don't we ride down there, boss? More cover for us.'

'Maybe so. But I prefer to be up here where I can see any sign of Littlejohn if he's on our trail already.' He spoke sharply to the other. Inwardly, he knew that the real reason why he wanted to remain where he was, on the trail, was that down in the narrow cut he had been assailed by a trapped feeling which he had not been able to throw off and which had grown stronger with every minute that passed. Besides, the sounds of hoofbeats on the rocky, hard-mud bottom would travel back along the canyon, channelled by the encroaching walls of rock and be picked up easily by a rider some distance away.

A quarter of a mile along the trail, they reined in among the rocks that lumped against the smooth dust of the narrow track. Leaning forward in their saddles, they listened intently. Sound would carry far in this wide, open country, Manvell knew. But he could hear nothing beyond the rustling sigh of the wind in the bunches of mesquite and the distant murmur of the sluggish river, still out of sight but not far from the trees. The rest of the land was silent.

Saunders asked: 'How much further before we make camp?'

'We'll ride on for a few more miles,' Manvell said thinly. 'I want to be among the trees before we rest up.'

'There's more cover there for Littlejohn to creep up on us after it's dark.'

'There's plenty of cover here too. Besides, he'll make more noise moving through the underbrush than he will sneaking up on us through the rocks.'

Wheeling his mount by pulling hard on the reins, he started on the slow upgrade of the trail. Here, the ground grew more rocky, more overgrown with thorn and mesquite and in several places the open country was cut up by large rocky upthrusts that interrupted their field of view.

'You sure that map you've got is right?' queried Saunders after they had ridden in silence for a while. 'This is bad country for men carrying any sort of weight.'

'It wasn't always as bad as this,' Manvell muttered. 'It's been nearly fifty years since they came this way. Things have changed in that time.' He jerked his head round sharply at a sudden movement. An antelope, startled by their approach, leapt into view, skidded sideways, throwing up a spurt of dust as it changed direction abruptly and went leaping out across an open stretch of ground. With an effort, Manvell forced himself to relax, steadying the rapid, thudding beat of his heart. He lowered the Winchester back into its scabbard. Beside him, Saunders had his rifle to his shoulders, but the antelope was away, out of reach of a killing shot before he could line it up for a proper aim. He thrust the weapon back again with a snort of disgust.

'We could've had fresh meat for supper,' he said harshly. 'Not too many of them left around here now.'

'Forget it. Won't be many places where we can light a fire anyway.'

'You mean we make cold camp?'

'You've done it before,' Manvell muttered harshly. 'What's one more time. Besides, you don't want Littlejohn creepin' up on you in the night, do you?'

Saunders twisted his thick lips into a snarl. 'If he did show up, it would be the last thing he did.'

'I wouldn't be too sure of that,' Manvell said warningly. 'You're fast with a gun, I'll admit. But from what I've heard of the gunfight between him and Ed Fazer, it was Ed who drew first and still Littlejohn beat him to the draw, and beat him handsomely. He's greased lightning with a gun, so if you want to stay alive, you'll do just as I say as far as Littlejohn is concerned. There are plenty of men in Boot Hill who thought they could beat Littlejohn in a straight draw.'

'We'll see about that later if the chance ever comes,' said Saunders dully. His small dark eyes looked far away. Manvell nodded slowly to himself. Some day this belief that he was better than most other men with a gun was going to be the end of Saunders. He hoped that whatever happened, the other would not do anything rash until they had the gold. Then Manvell had his own plans for the other and they did not include either sharing the loot with him or allowing him to accompany him over the border.

At the top of the rise, the ground levelled out and they

gave their mounts their heads. The timber rose in front of them close to the rising foothills, dark and green and shadowed. They had been out in the torturing, terrible heat of the sun most of the day and he would be glad to get into the green shade of those trees and rest up for the night. There was a deep weariness and a saddle soreness in his body which was beginning to tell on him. Saunders, sitting heavy in the saddle showed no sign of strain; his face set and fixed, eyes staring ahead. What kind of thoughts went on in that mind? Carrico wondered. Was the other aware of what lay in store for him once they found the gold? Did he, as yet, suspect that he might be shot in the back once his usefulness was finished? If he did, he showed no outward sign of it.

They pushed through a thick tangle of growth, their mounts straining hard against it as they thrust their way through. There was a small clearing where the rocky boulders lifted high all around it, a sort of circular depression some fifty yards across, then they were nearing the trees and a moment before they rode into them, Manvell reined up and twisted round in the saddle. The sun was going down now, very close to the horizon, and there was a battalion of creeping shadows over the uneven ground across which they had travelled. The faint sheen of the river was just visible off to his left and far away, maybe three or four miles in the distance, he thought he made out a cloud of dust, no bigger than a man's hand, dust which could have been raised by the hoofs of a fast moving horse.

Saunders stared out from beneath lowered brows as Manvell pointed a finger. He gave a ponderous nod. 'Looks like somebody pushin' his mount fast,' he agreed in answer to the mute look of inquiry on the other's face.

'It's Littlejohn, I'm positive of it,' Manvell said. 'I figured we might have thrown him off the trail, but no such luck. Maybe in the trees, if we cut away from the trail.'

They moved into the trees and the cool, aromatic air

swirled about them. Manvell was sweating now, even though the heat had been diminishing over the past three or four hours. He mopped his face with his sleeve. Half an hour passed as they moved deeper into the trees. Inwardly, Manvell knew that Littlejohn would be forced to slow his pace once he hit the timber. He would not dare to ride at any speed through the trees for fear of riding into an ambush. So he would feel his way forward very slow and careful; unless he decided to hole up for the night and wait until morning before he continued to trail them.

A quarter of a mile further on, the trail took a slow turn downward, but there was a narrower trail, little more than a game run, that angled off at this point, its beginning completely lost in the thick tangle of brush. Saunders was the one who spotted it, gestured towards it with his thumb. 'Could be we could make it along there,' he suggested. 'Make camp up in the higher reaches. Doubtful if Littlejohn will spot the entrance to that trail in the darkness by the time he gets here.'

'Now you're talkin' sense,' Manvell acknowledged. They edged their mounts into the brush and Manvell paused to lean back and draw some of the long snaking branches back into place, hiding the trail still further.

Their low fire was shielded by a rocky overhang which formed the smooth platform on which they found themselves into a sort of small cave where there was little fear of them being seen from above or below. The wind would carry the smoke of their fires away from the lower trail. Breaking out food and utensils from their saddle-bags, they sliced the salt bacon into a skillet and then put in the cold, boiled frijoles to warm alongside it. While it was frying, Manvell sent Saunders to scout the land around their camp. He had the urge to ensure that they could not be taken by surprise during the night. He had already made up his mind that they would take it in turn to sleep; that one of them would be awake all the time, watchful for trouble.

Saunders came back fifteen minutes later to report that everything was quiet. He sank down onto the hard smooth rock near the fire, held out his hands to its warmth for a moment and then helped himself to the food, piling it onto his plate and spooning it greedily into his mouth, eating ravenously in quick gulps as if he had not eaten a decent meal in days.

Manvell carried his plate over to the edge of the rocks, seated himself with his legs thrust out straight in front of him, his ears attuned to every little sound in the night. There was the faint, persistent rustling of nocturnal animals on the prowl in the brush and far off, the dismal wail of the coyote, rising and falling along a rasping scale. He felt a little shiver go through him at that doleful sound. It was the one noise he could never hear without feeling an eerie sense of utter loneliness.

Saunders finished his food, scraped the plate clean and then poured himself a mug of the boiling coffee which hung in the pot over the fire. He drank it noisily. Manvell felt the sound beginning to grate on his stretched nerves, was on the point of telling the other sharply to keep quiet, then thrust the quick retort away. There was no point in showing the other that he was all keyed up, tensed. It would have a bad effect on the man, might start giving him ideas of his own.

From beside the fire, Saunders called: 'Any sign of Littlejohn, boss?'

'Keep your voice down,' Manvell called back. 'Do you want him to know where we are?'

The other lapsed into a sullen silence, finished his coffee and placed the mug down on the rock beside him. He sat there for a long moment, then built himself a smoke, picked out a glowing ember on the blade of his knife with which to light the cigarette, then tossed it back into the fire again, drawing the smoke down into his barrel-like chest. He let his porcine eyes rest on Manvell's back for a long moment, thinking his own thoughts.

He was wondering just what it was that drove men to do things that Manvell was doing at that moment. He himself did not believe at all in this map which the other had got from Charlie Monroe. Everyone in town knew that Charlie had been weak in the head. That gold had either been found a long time before, or it would never be found. Besides, if the map was the real thing, where the hell had a man like Charlie Monroe got it from in the first place?

He got to his feet, walked over to where Manvell sat, lowered himself quietly onto the rock beside him. A deer crashed noisily through the undergrowth some distance below them, sending little echoes chasing themselves among the rocks, fading only slowly.

'He's stopped and bedded down for the night,' he said finally, his voice very soft. 'He won't risk tryin' to take us in the dark.'

'Even so, I've decided that we'll take it in turn to sleep. I'll keep the first watch.'

Saunders hesitated, then shrugged, saying nothing. He remained where he was for a few more minutes then, seeing that Manvell was in no mood for conversation, he moved back to the fire, tossed a few more dried branches onto it, stretched himself out in his blankets, listening to the snap of the flames as they ate along the wood.

Moodily, Manvell stared off into the darkness that lay all about him. In spite of the weariness in his body that pulled at every limb, his mind was curiously alert, and he knew that he would not have been able to sleep even if Saunders had offered to take the first watch. He fumbled for the map in his pocket, more to convince himself that it was still there than to try to check it in the faint flickering red glow from the fire. He kept an ear tuned to the country above the rocky overhang. It might be just like Littlejohn to circle around and ride the higher reaches, hoping to pick out something below him. The air cut cold at his back and he shivered, then got to his feet and moved back to the fire, squatting down beside it, poking at it absently with the toe of his boot. A shower of red sparks lifted high into the air until they were caught by the wind and whirled away. Lifting his gaze, he switched it to where Saunders lay in his blanket, snoring softly. Had he made a mistake bringing him along? Would he turn out to be more trouble than he was worth? Getting to his feet, he went over to the fire, bent and filled his cup with some of the coffee that was left. It had a bitter taste, but it brought some of the warmth back into his body.

When two hours had passed, he woke Saunders, went over to his own blankets and stretched himself wearily out on the hard ground. The snap and crackle of the fire sounded in his ears and he could hear the horses chomping softly in the distance. There was the high shrieking cry of a loon somewhere off in the trees and once, he thought he caught the faint, fading echo of a rider on the trail but the sound was distant and intermittent and he could not be sure. There was a whole host of criss-crossing trails here in the hills, many of them used by the outlaws who lived in this range and he had little fear that it had been Littlejohn moving over the lee of the foothills. The lawman would have bedded down by now. The thought of all that treasure waiting up there somewhere, at the spot marked on the map in his pocket, disturbed him anew and for several moments, he was worried by the thought that it might not be there now. After all, fifty years was a long time. A lot could have happened in that period. Somebody may have located it, without the aid of a map such as he now possessed.

The thought almost broke him in half as he lay there and he put it out of his mind with an effort. There was no sense in torturing himself with ideas like this. Another three or four days at the most and he would know whether his luck had held or not.

*

Ben Littlejohn had followed the trail of the two men until it was too dark for him to see it any further. They had made one or two half-hearted attempts to swing away from the main trail leading north, once or twice heading down into deep gullies and the dry creek bottoms, but he had had little difficulty in trailing them throughout the day. He had deliberately stayed well behind them, knowing that Manvell would be watching his rear throughout the day; not wanting to show himself.

When darkness had fallen, he had pulled his mount off the trail into the trees, made cold camp in a small clearing. Wind scoured down the hillside and once, turning in his blankets, he thought that he smelled smoke, drifting down on the wind from some higher level. If Carrico and the man with him had lighted a fire, they must have felt confident they were not being closely followed.

He was asleep almost instantly after that and when he woke it was already grey dawn and his horse was moving fitfully around in the brush. Eating some of the cold jerked beef he had brought with him, he washed it down with the ice-cold water from a nearby stream, then walked to the edge of the clearing where it looked down over a narrow rocky ledge onto the trail below him, studying his situation and looking about him. The trail made a long, slow sweep into denser timber a quarter of a mile further on the right hand wall blending into a sheer rock face for perhaps half that distance. Across the river, less than three hundred yards away, the rough, sloping shoulders of a ridge came down almost to the water's edge. He recalled having ridden this way earlier when he had first come to El Angelo, knew that among the trees, about a mile north of his present position, the river cut through the deep canyon, frothing and foaming over the rocks. The trail alongside the canyon at that point was a

96

rough one but passable; yet it ought to slow up those two men he was pursuing, and he doubted it they would have tried it during the night. Tricky by daylight, it would be far more dangerous in the dark and if they happened on any break or landslide, it could hold them up for some hours before they succeeded in finding a way around it.

As he pondered the situation, watching the grey dawn brighten slowly in the east, he built himself a smoke, leaned his back against a nearby tree. The only movement and sound came from a couple of woodchits that scurried upsidedown along one of the branches, scolding him for his presence there.

Finishing the smoke, he ground the butt out under his heel, walked back to his mount and threw the saddle on, tightening the clinch under the animal's belly, then mounted up after checking the Winchester in its scabbard.

As he edged his mount down onto the main trail once more, he wished that he knew this country so that he might strike over one of the bulging shoulders of the hills which could make it possible for him to move ahead of Manvell and take him without warning. The morning mists were lifting from the ground as he rode slowly among the trees. He kept a wary eye on the thick tangle of vegetation on either side of him and his right hand was never very far from the butt of the Colt at his waist.

Less than half an hour later, with the sunlight glinting down through the trees, he spotted the small trail that edged away from the main track. It was almost completely hidden by vegetation, but to his sharp eyes, it was clear that a horse had thrust its way through the under brush at that point and quite recently. The branches were bent back and the tall grass on the far side was flattened. He debated the proposition for a moment, then guessed that he had little to lose by investigating. A quick glance told him that there were no recent tracks in the dirt beyond the point where this trail turned off. So this was where the two men had made camp during the night. The narrow trail wound towards the higher ridges and he remembered the faint whiff of smoke that he had caught early the previous night drifting down from above him, brought down the slope by the night wind that sighed down from the summits. Less than fifteen minutes later, he came on the still warm embers of the fire built just beneath the rocky overhang. He spent precious minutes quartering the spot before he finally rode into the deserted camp. The two men had left about an hour before, he reckoned, and had not ridden down to the main trail, but had kept to the small game run, picking their way over some of the roughest country in the hills. Ben followed cautiously. The undergrowth here was so thick that he was several times forced to dismount and lead his horse forward and inevitably, he made more noise than he had intended.

Coming out into more open, through still rugged country, he scanned the ledges ahead of him for any sign of Manvell, but there was nothing. In the early morning sunlight, the trail which he had followed the previous day was just visible as a pale grey scar on the ground below him. It stretched away to the north along the rim of the steep-sided canyon for more than three miles before it dipped into timber again, and as far as he could see, it was empty. Then where were the two men? He sat forward in his saddle, hat tilted back on his head while random conjectures possessed his mind. There seemed no place they could have gone and he doubted if they had been able to move along that stretch of trail since dawn. Yet it was the only logical explanation.

A withered oak stood close to the trail as he put his mount at the downgrade. At some time in the past it had been struck and riven by lightning and now it was an excellent land-mark in this territory. He reined up close beside it, eyes speculative.

The next second, the sound of the single gunshot, barking from the rocks in the distance overlooking the trail, jerked him back in the saddle. The lead struck the tree within inches of his body. Instinctively, he jerked out of the saddle, drawing the rifle from its boot as he went down behind his mount, using the animal for cover. The marksman was less than two hundred yards away, he reckoned, crouched among the boulders high over the trail.

He cursed himself for not having realized the possibility of an ambush before. It was the sort of thing he could expect from Manvell. Maybe it was not Carrico himself up there. He would have ordered his companion to stay behind and ambush him, then ride on and catch up with him once the job was done. Gritting his teeth, he edged forward a few inches, risked a quick look between his mount's forelegs. Nothing moved up among the rugged boulders where he reckoned the gunman lay hidden, waiting for him to make another move. So long as the shots did not spook his mount, he was temporarily safe. But the next time, the gunslick might aim deliberately for his horse, knowing that if he killed or wounded the animal, he would be unable to follow them.

The other had chosen his position carefully, so that the sun was shining directly into Ben's eyes. Crouching tensely, he cast about him, noticed the narrow funnel in the rock immediately opposite him. He would have to run across the trail to reach it and risk getting a bullet in his body, but once he was down in its cover, he could worm his way upward until he was on the same level as the gunman. So long as he remained below the other, the man had the drop on him, could aim and fire between the rocks without really showing himself.

Steeling himself, he got his legs under him, hurled himself forward across the six feet of open space that separated him from the narrow gully. Two shots cracked out before he had thrown himself into the cover of the rocks. He heard the slugs strike the trail behind him, felt the wind of one of them as it scorched past his face. Then he was down, sobbing air into his heaving lungs, rolling forward as the gunman above him tried to spot him and fire again.

Now the tables were turning against the other. So long as Ben had been pinned down on the trail, the other was in a strong position. But now that he could no longer see him, could not tell accurately where he was, the advantage was passing slowly but surely to Ben.

The rocks closed in on him, crowding the narrow gully. It was a little more than a wrinkle in the ground where some past geological upheaval had caused the earth to give way and fold in on itself. Hugging the ground, he wormed his way up, keeping his head down. He had left the rifle back on the trail near his mount, knowing that soon he ought to be close enough to use his sixguns to their best advantage.

At the point where the narrow gully forked, he paused, listened intently. He could hear nothing, but he judged that he was now less than fifty yards or so from where the dry-gulcher lay hidden. The other would, he guessed, have his horse somewhere close by so that he could make good his escape if Ben happened to get too close to him. If only he could spot the gunman's mount and drop it or spook it along the trail, he would then be able to take his time with the man himself.

Moving with slow heaves of his legs, he went on, up the gully along the fork which angled in the direction of the loose jumble of rocks to his right. A moment later, he spotted the figure of the man who lay behind one of the upthrusting boulders. The other's rifle came up slowly to shoulder level and the man lifted his head cautiously, peering in all directions, trying to locate him. Ben smiled grimly. The other was getting nervous now, not sure of where he was and knowing that at any moment lead might start flying at him, cutting him down before he knew from where the danger might come. He slid one of the Colts from its holster, checked it swiftly, then glided forward over the loose shale and stones which formed the pathway here, his finger tightening a little on the trigger of the gun. The man was holed up some forty feet away, in a small hollow from where he could look down along the whole visible length of the trail. It was the ideal spot for an ambush.

For a moment, he debated whether to call the other. It was the honourable thing to do, but he put the idea out of his mind almost instantly. A dry-gulcher was the lowest form of vermin that a lawman ever came up against. He deserved everything he got.

Settling down behind a smooth-faced rock, he waited while the other moved his position, the wide-brimmed hat clearly visible. Squinting along the sights of the gun, resting the barrel on the side of the rock, Ben sighted and then squeezed off a shot. He saw the puff of powdered stone where the slug spanged from the rock an inch to the right of the other's head. The man pulled himself down smartly, remained out of sight.

Now the other knew where he was and he would either stay where he was and fight it out, or make a run for his horse. The issue was decided a few seconds later. From where he lay, Ben heard the scuffle of feet on the loose rock as the other shifted his position. For a moment, he caught sight of the man's bent figure between two of the tall boulders. But the other was moving fast and he was in sight for only a fraction of a second, not long enough for Ben to draw a bead on him with any real hope of hitting him.

He hesitated for only a moment, then ran forward, throwing caution to the winds, knowing that the other had decided to run for it; and that if he was to have a chance of nailing him, he would have to hit him before he reached his mount. There was no hope for Ben to get back to his own horse down on the trail in time.

Two shots rang out from the boulders as he raced forward. He dropped to his knees instinctively, heard them ricochet off the rocks some distance away, knew that the gunhawk was firing blind to keep him from closing up on him.

'Hold it right there, mister,' he yelled as he ran out into the narrow clearing that slanted over the ridges at right angles to that up which he had just climbed.

For a moment the running man hesitated, then swung sharply, loosed off a volley of shots before plunging out of sight. Something burned along Ben's arm, scorching along the flesh and the shock and surprise of it almost caused him to drop his gun. Grimly, he held on to it, raced forward. A moment later, he reached the end of the trail, almost plummeted down the precipitous slope where the ground fell sharply away in front of him for a distance of perhaps ten feet.

The clatter of hoofs on the rocky ground to his left brought him swinging sharply, but he was too late. He caught a fragmentary glimpse of the gunman spurring his mount into the coarse scrub that lined the trail twenty feet away. Then the man was round a sharply-angled bend in the trail and the sound of his flight died away into the distance until it was only a faint tattoo of sound, like the beat of fingers on a scrubbing board.

It was easy to see what had happened. The other's mount had been standing directly beneath the spot where Ben now stood and the gunman had simply dropped onto its back, raked spurs along its flanks and ridden off without wasting a second.

Disgustedly, he thrust his gun back into its holster. Making his way back to the trail, he swung up into the saddle of his horse, sat for a moment, and then thrust cartridges into the empty chambers. There was no sense in trying to catch up with the man who had just tried to kill him. The other had far too great a head start on him and would be riding the narrow arroyo trails which twisted and wound through the rocks and tangled undergrowth that lay thickly on the lower slopes of the hills. Whoever the other was, he knew these hills well, whereas if Ben tried to follow him he could loose himself within minutes. He decided to follow the main trail after Manvell.

Taking up the reins. he moved to dig spurs into his horse's flanks, then paused abruptly as he heard the run of an oncoming horse on the trail behind him.

SIX

BITTER JUSTICE

Ben listened to the horse come on at a swift run, then lifted the Winchester from its boot, levered a shell into the breech and held it, waiting, his eyes fixed on the trail where it wound out of the trees twenty feet away. Interest and natural caution rose together in his mind. Whoever it was, pushing their mount at that punishing pace, it was no ordinary rider along the hill trail. His first thought was that it might be one of the deputies, riding in from town with bad news. There flashed through his mind at that moment the knowledge that with him out of town, the men of the Triple C might band together and wipe out the riders working for Andrew Faulds, or even brace the town itself.

Sound and rider came quickly round the bend and out of the trees, heading towards him. He saw the other rein swiftly, the horse sliding to a halt less than ten feet away and he lowered the rifle with a faint shock of surprise.

'What are you doin' here, Alison?' he asked tightly.

The girl gave him a quick smile, brushed away a stray curl that fell over her forehead, escaping from beneath the wide-brimmed white hat she wore. 'Dan Thompson told me where you were headed and I thought you might like a little company. Besides, I've got a score to settle with Carrico

Manvell too. With Dad laid up with that shoulder, it's up to me to see that Manvell gets what's coming to him.'

'Now you know that this is no place for a woman,' Ben said firmly. 'These men are dangerous and they'll stop at nothin' to get this treasure.'

'I can handle a gun as well as any man,' she said stiffly. There was a trace of pride in her voice and the smile on her lips had tightened just a shade.

'I've no doubt you can, Alison,' Ben nodded. He urged his mount forward until he was just beside her, leaned over and put a hand on her arm. 'But one of them tried to gun me down from ambush only ten minutes ago. He'd have killed me too if he hadn't hurried his first shot. Now you see why I don't want you to come.'

Her lips were pressed tightly together now and he noticed the way her fingers gripped her reins more tightly. 'I'm still coming,' she said harshly. 'This is something to do with me as well as with you. You want to see that the law is upheld. I want to see that justice is carried out.'

'Justice, Alison,' said Ben softly. 'Or revenge?'

He saw the faint flush that rose unbidden to her cheeks and thought how beautiful she looked when she was really angry as she was at that moment. 'All right then. Call it revenge if you like. But Manvell has done everything he could to destroy my father, the ranch, everything we own.'

Ben gave a quick nod. 'I know just how you feel. But that's why I'm here. When I catch up with him, he'll come back to El Angelo with his hands tied behind him and he'll stand trial.'

'In front of Judge Chandler?' There was naked scorn in the girls voice. 'You don't think he'll be convicted do you, even if you've got the best kind of proof against him. Everyone in town is afraid of Carrico Manvell. The judge is in cahoots with him. Together they run this territory. Nothing will stop Manvell but a bullet.'

'It may possibly come to that in the end,' Ben said slowly. Inwardly, he felt sure that Manvell would never allow himself to be taken alive, not with all of that gold and silver at stake. He would fight like a wounded, cornered wildcat.

'Then I can ride with you.' He thought he detected a note of pleading in her tone now, although the look of determination was still on her face.

Ben hesitated, then chuckled. 'Very well. But you do exactly as I tell you. Do you know the kind of coyotes I'm trailin'?'

'Yes,' she said. She looked long at him, something half formed on her lips and in her eyes. Giving a faint smile, he saw caution hold her back. 'I know these men.'

'And you're not afraid?'

'All I want is to see them dead.' There was a rising hardness in her now. For a moment he stared at her in surprise, saw her drop her gaze before his probing look.

'I don't like to hear hardness in a woman,' he said softly. 'But I guess that you have reason enough to be hard.' Swinging sharply on the reins, he pulled his horse's head around and they rode at a quick trot along the trail, cutting up towards the thickening scrub that formed a thin boundary between the rocky ground and the dense timber.

Five minutes they were among the trees. Here, thought Ben, looking cautiously about him, it was like being in some deeply-vaulted church, with the sunlight turned yellow and green by the thick canopy of branches and leaves overhead. Most of the way, they formed an impenetrable layer above the trail so that they seemed to be riding along a huge tunnel with the thick carpet of pine needles which had fallen over the years, muffling the sound of their horses.

'Do you know this country?' Ben asked after a while.

The girl gave him a quick, sideways glance. 'I know most of it,' she conceded. 'I was raised here, rode these trails with my father before I grew up and he decided that I ought to get an education back East. I used to love these forests and hills. In those days, there was peace here even though we were right on the frontier. You could ride without having to watch your back for fear of being shot down without warning. There was little, if any, rustling. The town was building itself up and you could walk without fear down the main street even after dark. But since Carrico Manvell and his hired killers rode in, that has been impossible. Those days are gone now, and there are many of us who wonder if they'll ever come back.'

'They will,' Ben affirmed. 'But these things have to be fought for now. The townsfolk and the smaller ranchers have let things slide to a dangerous degree. They can't hope to get the good old days back without some sacrifices. Maybe if they'd stepped in at the very beginning, they might have had a good chance; but not now.'

'Do you really blame them so much?' she asked sombrely.

Ben drew back into his thoughts for a moment, then shrugged. 'Maybe it is hard to lay all the blame on them. A man always tries to take the easy way out whenever there's trouble brewin'. He tries to tell himself that if he doesn't stir up more than there is, it will all sort itself out in time. Unfortunately, that isn't the way of it. Evil grows and flourishes on evil. It's been that way ever since the world began and it will always go on that way. A strong man has to stand up to evil and force it to back down.'

'And you think that you're that man?'

'You asked me that question once before,' he reminded her. 'Like I told you then, I think so. Anyway there's nobody else. When I took this job of Town Marshal, I made it a condition that the town would back me in any play I had to make. Somehow, I don't think they'll keep their promise.'

'They're afraid. They have families and so far, Manvell hasn't gone against the ranchers.' She let out a long sigh. There was a momentary stiffness on her face which she could not hide.

They came to a summit of the trail. In front of them, it dipped downward across a long, open stretch of country full of gullies and ravines that showed dark shadow in the strong sunlight. Suddenly, the girl stiffened in the saddle, caught at his arm then pointed off into the distance.

Ben narrowed his eyes, caught the movement far off, perhaps a mile and a half away, the cloud of dust that marked a fast-moving rider. He drew his lips together in a grim smile.

'That's the *hombre* who tried to bushwhack me,' he said firmly. 'He's ridin' hard to catch up with Manvell. Could be that he knows about the gold and the map that Carrico is carryin' on his person and he suddenly doesn't trust the other any more. Maybe he's even got ideas of grabbin' off that treasure for himself.'

'When thieves distrust each other and fall out . . . .' murmured the girl softly, her words so quiet that he could only just make them out.

Saunders caught up with Carrico Manvell shortly after mid-afternoon. The other had ridden far and fast since morning, had progressed much further than Saunders had anticipated and he had almost given up hope of finding the other before nightfall when he came upon him on the bank of a narrow, swift-running stream. Carrico was bending over the water, drinking thirstily and letting it trickle over his face and neck, rubbing at his sun-scorched skin with his bandanna soaked in the cool water. He was on his feet, swinging round, his gun out and covering the other before Saunders had reached him.

'Hold it there, boss,' called Saunders urgently. He slid from the saddle and led his mount forward. 'You're almighty quick with that gun of yours. You might have plugged me without givin' me a chance.'

'Sorry,' said the other tightly. He let the gun drop back into his holster. 'I didn't know who you were. For all I knew,

Littlejohn might have killed you and it could have been him on my trail.'

Saunders said nothing, but got down onto his knees on the river bank and drank his fill, the water dripping from his chin as he lifted his head. Then he took out his water bottle and filled it to the brim before getting back onto his feet.

After a moment of silence, Manvell said harshly: 'Well, did you get him?'

Slowly, the other shook his head. 'He's too goddamned fast. He was ready for trouble. I figure he spotted me before I could get a bead on him. He came after me among the rocks so I lit out.'

'And he's still trailin' us?' There was a note of thinly disguised anger in Manvell's tone. He faced the other down with a hard stare. 'I should have known better than give you the chance of gettin' him. But you reckoned you were so fast with a gun that you could take him easily.'

'We didn't meet on even terms,' said the other defensively. 'I was hemmed in among the rocks and he could've come at me from any direction. I didn't fancy the idea of bein' plugged in the back.'

'So you ran like a scared rabbit,' sneered the other.

Saunders brought his bull-like head up. There was an ugly look on his face and his hand moved suggestively towards the gun at his waist. Manvell saw the slight movement, said through his teeth, 'Just make a move for that gun, Saunders, and it'll be the last thing you do.'

There was a cold, deadly menace in his words, but for a second, the thought of action lived in the other's eyes. Then he forced himself to relax, let his hand fall to his side, shrugged and turned away back towards his horse.

A grim little smile played around the edges of Manvell's lips for a moment as he watched the other move away. He had known all the time that Saunders would back down, fast as he was. Moving over to a rock, he seated himself on it and took out the map, spreading it out on his knee, pouring over it as he traced the trail which they had taken so far. He was reasonably certain that they were still on the right route. They had passed the bend in the river which was clearly marked late that morning and he figured that the stream by which they were now stopped was the one marked in red near the middle of the map. About two miles further on, if they were following the right trail, there was a deep, unmistakable canyon that would lead them away from the foothills and further into the more desolate country inside the range of mountains.

From near the water's edge, Saunders watched him curiously. He had been wondering about that map for a long time now, ever since he had heard that Charlie Monroe had been shot at Felipe's place. He walked over to the other, noticed the way in which Manvell folded the piece of paper and thrust it into his pocket the moment he saw him approaching.

'Somethin' on your mind, Saunders?' Manvell asked tersely.

'Just wonderin' why we're headed into this country lookin' for buried gold if it's only that map of Monroe's you're followin'.'

'What do you know of this map?' Carrico demanded.

Saunders stared belligerently at him for a moment, then squatted down. He said thinly: 'What if there were folk from San Miguel and they came and dug it up some time ago.'

'They didn't,' Manvell said quickly, his tone rising a little in pitch.

'Sure, but how do you know?' persisted the other.

'Because I do,' snapped the other. 'This ain't no time for you to come up with ideas like that. Another two days and we'll be near the spot where they buried it. Then it's all ours.'

'Just askin' an idle question,' said the other slowly. His gaze never left Manvell's face. 'What about the rest of the boys back at the Triple C? Do they get a share of it?'

Manvell laughed shortly. 'Why should they? Split among

them and nobody would get anythin' worth talkin' about. I figure that the two of us make enough to share.'

'And the Triple C? You mean to leave that to run itself?'

Manvell grinned. 'Ain't really no cause to worry none about the place. I built it up from nothin'. Besides, I reckon that I might be able to get word through to the judge to dispose of it for me and take the money south into Mexico. That will be chicken-feed compared with what we'll get for the treasure.'

Saunders glanced at him slyly. 'Sometimes, I get the idea that you mean to keep it all for yourself.'

'Why should you figure that?' Manvell eyed him narrowly. He could see that the other was beginning to get suspicious and it was important to allay any fears the other might have in that direction at least until they had found the gold. He might even let the other come with him all the way to the Mexico border as an additional safeguard against Ben Littlejohn. Once they were across into Mexico he would have no compunction about shooting the other in the back the first opportunity he got. But he knew he would also have to keep a watchful eye on Saunders. There was no way of telling what kind of thoughts were running through the other's mind.

Saunders pulled in a deep breath. Taking out his long-bladed knife, he began whetting it on a nearby piece of sandstone. 'Tellin' me to stay back there and ambush Littlejohn. My guess is you could have figured that he'd kill me. That would leave you to go on and get everything for yourself.'

'You're talkin' just like Littlejohn would want you to talk,' Manvell said tightly. 'We have to do this thing together or we're both finished. Littlejohn won't give up easy. He'll follow us all the way and the only way we can rid ourselves of him is to kill him. Don't you see that? You're good with a gun. I reckoned you'd have a good chance to plug him if you took him by surprise. Could be that you had a bit of bad luck. The next time he won't be so fortunate. I promise you.'

The sunlight, reflected bluely from the blade of the knife as the other worked it steadily and smoothly over the stone, flashed in his eyes and he blinked them several times. He knew that his nerves were beginning to become frazzled, stretched as taut as wires throughout his body. He knuckled at the sand and dust that clogged his mouth and nostrils. As he sat there, straining to listen and separate fact from fancy, he tried to forget his physical discomfort, telling himself that another few days and he could say goodbye to all of this, that he could get as much money in that short time as he would get in a lifetime of working the Triple C ranch, even if he had managed to get his hand on all of the other spreads about him.

'You hear anythin'?' Saunders asked after a pause.

'Nothin' yet.'

'He can't be too far behind us. Unless he's decided to swing across the hills in the hope of boxing us in against the trail.'

'He won't try that,' said Manvell with conviction. 'He knows nothing of this country and he won't want to run the risk of losing us. He'll stick to this trail all the way.'

Leaving the stream, they pushed on, still heading north. During the afternoon, the wind lifted, blowing the scudding sand into their faces. The towering hills did little to soften the impact of the easter as it swept along the wide valley between the ranges. Within minutes of it starting it had become a sand-laden gale that scoured and abraded, tearing at their flesh, a burden to both man and beast. The shrill gusts bent the rattling mesquite, whipped the low branches of the trees into a fury, hurling the feathery fronds at their shoulders as they rode beneath them.

Bent low in the saddle, Saunders grumbled continuously as the dust beat at him. It was virtually impossible to see anything while the gale lashed at them and they were forced to lead their horses in several places where the trail narrowed and there was the risk of going over the edge at the first wrong move.

'We've got to find shelter from this storm,' Saunders yelled harshly, moving closer to Manvell to make himself heard above the scouring, shrieking wind.

Manvell shook his head. The sand was cutting at him as much as at the other, but he shouted back: 'We go on, Saunders. We can't afford to stop – not yet.'

'Don't be such a goddamned fool. If we stay out in this much longer, it'll shred all of the flesh off our bones. I've ridden in these sandstorms before, Carrico. I know what they can do to a man after an hour or so.'

'Never mind that. It won't stop Littlejohn. You can take your choice, a bad pounding from the storm or a bullet from him.'

Saunders rubbed the back of his sleeve over his face, grunted harshly, but continued to plod forward, body bent into the wind, leading his mount on a short rein.

They reached a long, jagged shelf of ground an hour later. The sun was now totally obscured by the flying clouds of dust and sand, and only a pale reddish glow gave any indication of its position in the sky. Eyes squeezed shut to mere slits, the men struggled forward. Their features were now raw and bleeding where the scudding grains of sand had torn at their flesh, their mouths and nostrils were clogged by it. The millions of tiny granules were everywhere, working their way into eyes and ears and nose, down between their clothing and their body, irritating and painful. The horses were in a similar condition. Heads bent so low that they almost touched the ground, they seemed to be moving forward by sense of smell and touch rather than by sight. Not that it was possible to see much anyway. The swirling, vaporous clouds of yellow dust obliterated many except the closest details and for the past half hour, the men had seen little beyond the

113

rough, uneven ground beneath their feet.

Movement was a nightmare of mental and physical discomfort. Saunders continued to mutter under his breath, staring around at Manvell now and again through red, inflamed eyes. His hair was plastered down against his forehead with sweat, matted with the yellow dust and the mask of sand on his face gave him a diabolical appearance, with only his slitted eyes showing any sign of life. Manvell knew that the other's features were merely a mirror image of his own.

Crossing a patch of broomweed, they staggered into a wide cleft in the sheer wall of rock that had run alongside the trail in an unbroken ridge for more than a mile. Knuckling the dust from his eyes, Manvell looked about him, turning his head slowly. There was something about this place that nudged a little memory in his mind, but several seconds passed before he realized the significance of it.

This was the place marked on the map, the landmark telling them that here they moved off the main trail, going deeper into the hinterland. He motioned to Saunders, pointing into the shadowed outcrops of rock that loomed high over them. 'That way,' he yelled harshly.

For a moment the other stared at him dully. 'You sure?' he asked. 'That trail leads into a cul-de-sac. There ain't no way out if we go up there. Littlejohn can box us in if he follows along that trail.'

'We go accordin' to the map,' Manvell said gratingly.

Saunders turned his head, peered through heavy-lidded eyes as though seeing an invisible puzzle up in the swirling clouds of dust. Then he shrugged his shoulders ponderously, moved off the trail. Climbing into the saddle, he said grimly. 'Be damned if I'm walkin' up that way, draggin' this horse with me.'

Manvell swung up too, urged his mount forward. For a moment the animal shied away from the line of tumbled rocks that blocked the exit from the trail, then jumped them, following Saunders. The wind covered all sounds except the cracking rasp of the mesquite and thorn. Tumbleweed drifted over the rocks and scudded like living creatures into the shadows. Their mounts moved upward with laboured breathing, fighting to maintain their balance on the treacherous ground.

The narrow gully widened after a while, but it still wound and twisted a tortuous way up the face of the mountain. No trees grew along these open, weatherbeaten ridges and there was no shelter from the wind and sand. Manvell felt as if his whole body had been clawed by a wildcat and knew that there was blood on his face too where the skin had been roughened and torn.

In spite of the pain, eagerness continued to ride him and gold hunger was stronger than any other emotions, stronger than food hunger or weariness. Their horses could move no faster than a man's walk now and he was still a little apprehensive about Littlejohn following their trail. Sooner or later, argued the little voice at the back of his mind, the marshal was going to catch up with them; that much was inevitable. Saunders had tried to stop him once, and had failed. That would put Littlejohn on his guard now and he doubted if any further attempt to ambush him would work.

Shortly before sundown, the storm abated almost as quickly as it had risen and there was a vivid red glow in the west, like the fires from some mighty explosion beyond the rim of the world. The air became cooler, felt like a benison against their burned faces, the sky cleared and blinking his eyes, the eyeballs feeling as though they had been scratched over the entire surfaces, he searched the banks of red sandstone on either side of the gully intently, but they went on for another half mile or so before he spotted the cut which their horses could climb quite easily. The animal dug in to his spurring and struggled over the loose shale, legs straight, until it came out on a cedar stand where it stood blowing noisily, thankful for the chance to rest.

Stepping down, he moved to the edge and peered down. Saunders was coming up the narrow wrinkle in the ground, cursing his stumbling mount. He drew level with Manvell, rubbed at his face where the sweat, trickling down from his forehead had mixed with the sand, itching and irritating.

'Goddamned trail,' he said thickly. He spat into the brush nearby, trying to clear his mouth of the clogging dust. 'You sure this is the right way? Can't see how those other *hombres* got up here carrying all that loot.'

'They made it all right,' Manvell said tightly. He moved away from the lip of the rocky shelf, sat down with his back against a dead cedar stump and munched on the food from his saddle-bag. Now that the wind had died, there was an awe-inspiring stillness over everything; a silence that hemmed them in and crowded down from the uplifted horizons. It was a ghostly silence that made his nerves shriek. With an effort, he pulled himself together. He did not want to think about ghosts at that particular moment. He remembered Charlie Monroe and the other men he had killed, tried to rub out the memory of them too. Damn it, he thought savagely, he had seen a whole host of men die. There was no reason why he should be afraid of them now. The dead were unable to harm anybody and it was the living, men like Ben Littlejohn, he ought to fear.

'Any sign of that marshal?' asked Saunders.

Manvell shook his head. 'That dust storm. It may have blotted out our trail. Even if he follows into the fork yonder, it's doubtful if he'll head this way. Ain't nothin' to lead him up here with all of our prints rubbed out by the wind.'

'Could be that storm did us a good turn then,' grunted the other. He took off his boots, emptied the yellow sand from them. 'Where are you figurin' on spendin' the night? This country looks all the same to me. Besides, the horses are real tuckered out. They won't go much further.'

'All right. We'll make camp here.' Manvell stared levelly at the other for a long moment. The going had been tough for most of the day, really tough, and the fact that in several places they had been forced to dismount and lead their horses forward, had wearied them more than usual. He was glad himself, to be able to rest. His bones were weary, his flesh torn and bruised. Getting to his feet, he led his mount up the trail a piece, tethered it to the shattered stump of a tree, giving it plenty of rope so that it might graze on the tough, coarse grass which grew around the base of the tree.

Going back, he found that Saunders was trying to start a fire with twigs and bits of wood he had collected. Angrily, Manvell stamped it out, whirled on the other. 'Don't you know better than to light a fire here?' he said through his teeth. 'You'd signal to Littlejohn exactly where we are. That smoke could be seen for miles from up here.'

'Goddamnit!' snarled the other. 'You mean that we have to squat here in the cold through the night after the beatin' we took from that storm?'

'Better that than have Littlejohn creepin' up on us durin' the night. Now you'll do just as I say or you can take your mount and head right back to town. I'm bossin' this deal – and don't you forget it or try to step out of line again.'

Saunders sat where he was, his head thrown back, his eyes narrowed as he glared up at the other. His tone was icy as he said: 'Just what is it that you want, Manvell. I've worked for you for close on two years now, done all you asked me to do. But this gold seems to have gone to your head.'

Manvell stopped still. His right hand hovered dangerously close to his gun butt. 'Like I just said, I give the orders. There's enough wealth buried up in these hills to make the two of us rich men for the rest of our lives. Ain't no sense in thrown' that away, is there?'

'All right,' mumbled the other. He took out his hunting knife, tested the blade on the ball of his thumb. 'But just quit ridin' me all the time, that's all. I don't like it. Besides, I've only got your word that there is any loot buried in this spot you keep talkin' about.'

'And that's all you're likely to have until we get there,' Manvell opened his bedroll, laid it out on a smooth patch of rock. They weren't going to sleep in much comfort during the night, but it couldn't be helped.

The sun had dropped out of sight now below the western horizon and the sky was clear above their heads as if the driving sand had scoured and washed it clean. There were no clouds except for a few low down in the west, still touched with the bright crimson of the fading sunset. Stretching himself out on the ground he chewed on a strip of jerky, raising himself occasionally onto one elbow to glance over the rim of the rocky shelf, straining to pick out any movement down in the direction of the main trail.

The easter had struck at Ben and the girl while they were working their way along the bank of the river and, more fortunate than Manvell and Saunders, they were protected to a certain extent by the sweeping fold of the rising foothills which shielded them from the full fury of the storm. Nevertheless, they had caught some of it and although Ben would have liked to have rested up in the heavy timber close to the trail, the girl would have none of it. She knew, instinctively, that had it not been for her presence there, Ben would have continued on the trail without a thought of stopping because of the storm and she was determined that she would be no burden to him. She had ridden after him of her own accord, and it was up to her to ensure that nothing she did would slow him down or force him to give up his mission of tracking down these two killers.

They stayed with the main trail upward and it took them presently out of the protective timber and into the rougher country where they were forced to ride with their heads bowed as the sand was hurled at them along the valley. For more than an hour, they progressed slowly. Then the wind died, they were able to make better time, although it was now virtually impossible for them to follow the trail of the two men.

The timber when they entered it, was old first-growth pine and cedar, smooth and massive at the butt, rising in a flawless line to the thick canopy overhead that blotted out most of the late evening light. There was little underbrush here and in places, where the trees thinned, they were able to see for more than half a mile in either direction. The stillness of the foothills lay on everything, until only the harsh breathing of their horses broke the silence.

It would only be a matter of time before Manvell cut away from the trail, Ben reflected and they would have to keep their eyes open for any likely spot. He had ridden this main trail all the way from the north when he had come to El Angelo, knew most of the places through which it wound, and also that it was unlikely that any treasure would be hidden close by it. Those monks from the monastery of San Miguel would have chosen a more secluded and inaccessible spot than any he had seen on his southward ride.

The smooth, red-barked trees ran before them for another quarter of a mile, and then the trail lifted suddenly upward and the country roughened abruptly. It was as if nature had decided that two vastly different types of country could exist side by side and was determined to show it. Here, in the open, with the sun down below the western horizon, the air was blue-shadowed and still, with a soothing coolness that sighed down from the higher slope. They were breaking free of the trees when Ben heard the fading echo, far away and up among the high ridges. The sound of a horse among rocks. Pausing, he listened for its repetition, but he heard nothing more.

The girl had heard the faint sound too, for she turned her

head, holding it a little on one side. 'Did you hear that?' she asked quietly.

He nodded. 'It could have been anything,' he said harshly. 'Sound can be deceptive in these hills. It could have been miles away or just around the next bend.'

'But it was a horse being ridden,' persisted Alison.

He nodded briefly in agreement. Already, his mind was racing on, assessing events, rejecting ideas that came into his mind, trying to put himself into Carrico Manvell's place, trying to outguess him. 'Let's keep movin',' he said harshly. 'I want to catch up with them before it's completely dark if I can. By now, they'll be holed up someplace, off the main trail. If we don't find them by nightfall we'll lose them.' He eyed her closely with a studying glance for a moment. 'Think you can make it, Alison?'

She smiled bravely. 'I'm sure I can, Ben,' she answered. 'Just you lead the way.'

They stayed within shelter for as long as possible, then rose with the short, sharp switchback courses that began to lift them up in the side of the mountain. The daylight slowly faded but now that the storm had passed and the sky was clear, it lingered longer than he had anticipated earlier that afternoon. They were still pointed towards the summits of the far end of the range when they reached the point in the trail where the shrieking wind had whipped the sand over the narrow trail, obliterating everything. Ben shrugged his shoulders philosophically. From this point on, they were trailing the two killers blind, at least until they picked up the trail again, and knowing Manvell he would have taken very great care to see that this was made as difficult as possible for them.

Pausing to water their mounts by the small, swift-running stream, they pushed on into the growing gloom. Within fifteen minutes, the trail brought them to a point where a wide cut splayed up into the rocky ground, twisted several times before it vanished completely from sight. There was little vegetation on the steep slope, a few tufts of grass and mesquite but that was all. Ben reined up his mount and pondered the situation seriously. This was the first spot they had reached where there was a definite choice confronting the two men they were pursuing. Either they had continued on along the trail, or they had swung off at this point and headed up into the higher ridges.

The main trail was undoubtedly the better way of moving through these hills. But that, as he saw it, was not the point. Manvell was not a free man, able to choose the trail he would take. He would be slavishly following the directions given in that map he had killed for and he would want to get off the main trail as soon as he could. Dismounting, he handed the reins to the girl and walked forward to the end of the cut. Bending, he studied the ground closely, walking forward slowly at the same time, eyes searching for some sign that would tell him whether Manvell had come this way or not.

Ten yards inside the wide wrinkle of ground, he found what he was looking for. The piece of cloth had been snagged on an out-thrusting twig. He picked it off, and examined it carefully.

'What have you got there?' called Alison in a quiet voice.

He went back to her. 'Looks like a piece of somebody's shirt. I'd say they cut up there just after the storm.'

'Do we go up after them?' She looked fully at him, placing a hand on his arm. 'It will be simple for them to lay another ambush for us up there.'

'I know. But that is a chance I shall have to take. If I can stop them now, I can get that map back. I want you to stay down here. I doubt if they went very far before makin' camp and—'

'I want to come with you.' As she spoke, the girl slid the Winchester from the saddle boot, held in her hand. She laid her glance on Ben, her lips pressed tightly together, defying him to stop her.

Inwardly, he knew that it would be useless to try, yet his desire to keep her out of danger was uppermost in his mind. 'Try to see things my way, Alison,' he said softly. 'I don't want to put you in any danger at all. These men are killers, both of them, and they won't stop at shootin' a woman. Could be they'd shoot you first, in the hope of makin' me give in. That's the reason I don't want you up there with me if I bump into them. I wouldn't feel free to act as I must, if I knew you were there, invitin' them to plug you.'

'But you'd risk your own life to take on the two of them,' she pointed out logically. 'I'm not afraid to use this rifle on them.'

'Somehow, I doubt if you'd be able to pull the trigger and shoot down a man in cold blood, even if you knew you had to, to save your own life. This is my job, what I've known for more years than I care to remember.'

He saw her harden against his suggestion and had an instant answer. 'I was brought up out here in these hills, Ben. I know the kind of coyotes who run here, animals and men. I've got no regrets for the townsfolk who let Manvell ride in and take over, riding roughshod over them. But when it comes to rustling our cattle, then I want to take a hand in it.'

'There's hardness in you, Alison,' he said, and knew he had told her that before.

'You disapprove?'

'Not exactly. Maybe a man wants a woman to be somethin' different to himself. Maybe he wants to see softness in her.'

He saw her quick smile. She laid a hand on his arm, said very gently: 'You know, Ben. I think that's the most revealing thing you've ever said since I met you. You're not one man, but two.'

He opened his mouth to say something more, then closed it again, moved over to his horse and mounted up. 'Whatever you do, keep under cover if we do run into any trouble. Do I have your promise on that?'

She nodded. 'If it will make you feel any happier.' She rode alongside him as they put their tired mounts to the steep upgrade, watching him quietly out of the corner of the side of her vision. He was sitting taller in the saddle now, more tensed, full of the knowledge that there was danger ahead on this particular trail, that it could strike at any moment and from any direction. She also knew that he was inwardly worried and concerned for her safety, and she felt an unaccustomed warmth in her which she could not, at that moment, explain. It was like nothing she had experienced before and she fell to wondering about it for a little while, striving to analyse her own feelings about this man who watched the rocks on either side of them with a kind of restless attention, his hand very close to the gun at his waist. He had a great deal of assurance about him, she thought to herself, no doubt in his own abilities. And she felt sure that behind the hardness which drove him, there was a great personal gentleness and warmth. His infrequent, slow smiles had a great effect on her.

They rode slowly into the night wind that began to sigh off the summits. She rubbed her face with her sleeve, noticed the yellow-white dust that came off her skin.

Riding a few feet in the lead, Ben maintained a watchful alertness, scanning the dark shadows on either side, noticing how the oncoming night drowned out most of the light now, made it difficult to see detail in the rough country through which they were riding. More than once, since they had started up from the trail it had occurred to him that maybe Manvell had been more clever than he had figured; that maybe he had deliberately snagged that piece of cloth onto that bush to throw him off the scent and sent him out along the wrong trail. In the growing darkness he could see no sign of prints in the dusty patches that lay between the huge boulders; but this was bad country for showing sign and he knew that this meant very little. So, not altogether free from doubt, he turned a sharply-angled bend in the trail, spotted the point some fifty feet ahead where the ground levelled off. The cliff at this point was bare rock and dirt, with only a little dry, stiff vegetation clinging precariously to the small patches of earth, sucking an existence from the arid soil. His mount was both tired and doubtful, stopping at intervals to look about it, needing to be prodded ahead with a touch of the rowels on its flanks.

He had gone another fifteen feet when the horse stopped again and this time it refused to heed the spurs, would not go on. Bending forward in the saddle, he peered down at the earth in front of him, thinking that perhaps there was a fresh slide of dirt here. The animal began to gather its legs together, made a lot of little mincing steps, turning full circle.

'What is it?' whispered the girl. She had reined up her own mount when his had halted. Now she was glancing at him curiously in the gloom.

'I'm not sure. The trail still seems to be there. Could be that—' He broke off instantly, caught the girl's arm and pulled her back sharply behind the rock as the rifle shot rang out from the boulders forty feet or so away. He saw the sharp orange stiletto of light from the muzzle of the weapon, heard the vicious whine of the slug as it spanged off the rock a couple of inches away.

'Get down,' Ben hissed. 'They're holed up in the rocks yonder. They must've spotted us comin' along the trail and waited until we got within range.'

'Can you see them?'

'No, they're keepin' their heads down.' He drew their horses back into the rocks, then moved back to where the girl was crouched down behind the rock. She had pulled her Winchester from the boot and was now holding it in her hands.

Another bullet broke the open ground ahead of them and a third one smashed splinters of rock off the edge of the boulder just above his head. The girl flinched slightly and drew back. Bending forward, Ben tried to catch an upward glimpse at the rim of rocks in the distance but found his field of vision much too limited. Picking up a twig, he placed his hat on top of it, lifted it slowly above the rim of the boulder. The marksman's shot came almost at once and when he pulled it down again, there was a neat hole bored through the crown of the hat.

He smiled grimly across at the girl. 'Nothin' wrong with his aim,' he said tautly. Checking his weapon, he said: 'Keep me covered from here, but don't show yourself any more than necessary. They may not know that you're with me. If they reckon I'm still alone, we may be able to take them by surprise.'

He saw the girl's quick nod of understanding, then edged back behind the rocks, working his way down to a spot he had marked previously where it was possible for a man to worm his way between the tall granite boulders without too much difficulty.

More shots cracked out from the distant rocks and he hoped that nothing would happen to the girl. If it did, he swore that he would trail Manvell and his crew to the end of the world to get even with them. The force of his feelings was such that he was on the spot where the two boulders crushed together almost before he realized it. Squirming between them, feeling his clothing scrape against the rough rock, he stepped cautiously through, listening to the volume of rifle fire in the distance and trying to gauge where it was coming from, whether the two gunmen had shifted their position. The well-spaced, methodical shots from the girl's Winchester continued and he felt a wave of relief wash through him, knowing that she was still all right.

Jagged rocks scraped at him fiercely as he forced his way up. In the darkness he was forced to rely on his sense of touch more than that of sight, but eventually he came over the lip of the high boulder, clinging to precarious handholds, shinning around crumbling rock outcrops, using all of the shortcuts he could find in order to work his way around Manvell's position. Time was running at a high premium, he knew. At any moment, one or other of the men might decide to move forward and if they found only the girl there, she would not stand a chance against these killers.

The thought drove him to take a few extra chances now, looking up ahead all the time, choosing the best path he could find up the side of the mesa, making full use of the twisting, grotesque fissures he found there. By the time he had squirmed up onto a narrow ledge, he was winded, his fingers torn and bleeding from the knife-edged rocks and he threw himself down in the coarse grass that grew there in ragged tufts.

Crawling swiftly, his Colt in his right hand, he moved slantwise over the face of the mesa, until he was crouched in a cleft of rock that looked down onto the wide cutting along which Manvell and his companion had travelled. He could just make out the wide, level plateau with the tumble of rocks fronting it, less than thirty feet away and almost on the same level as himself. The next instant, he spotted the twin stilettos of orange flame that showed among the rocks, pinpointing for him the positions of the two men. He angled a little, moving in a wide arc so that he could edge a little higher than them, could just make out their shapes lying flat on their bellies, aiming their Winchesters down the slope.

Carefully, he sighted his gun on the nearer of the two men. For a second, it came to him that he was doing something he had never done before, shooting down a man from cover, without giving the other an even chance. But he dismissed the faint feeling of guilt almost at once. These men were killers, they had no compunction in shooting down a man from ambush, one of them had tried it earlier with him. He took up the trigger's slack, fired a shot at the man, saw the figure jerk as the slug hit him.

Instantly, both men had rolled back out of sight. Their reactions to danger had been swift, far quicker than Ben had expected. His next two shots whined off the rocks, forcing the men to keep their heads down and relieving the fire against the girl.

From below, the girl continued to fire at the rocks, then stopped. In the sudden stillness that ensued, a harsh voice called: 'That you there, Littlejohn?'

'That's right, Manvell. Now step out of there with your hands lifted where I can see you.'

'Why don't we just talk this over,' answered the other hoarsely. 'I've got the map and there's plenty of gold and silver buried there for all of us. Another couple of days and we could be rich men. Just how much do you reckon to get on a Town Marshal's pay?'

'You don't seem to have got the point, Manvell. I'm takin' you in for the murder of Charlie Monroe and any others you've gunned down in cold blood in the past. The same goes for your companion who tried to ambush me along the trail.'

'You'll never take us,' snarled a new voice which he did not recognize. A second later, vicious red streaks blossomed in the night and he heard the deadly whine of bullets humming through the air close to his head.

Ben squeezed his trigger, sent shots whistling down into the darkness, aiming for the muzzle flashes. The flash of his own gun half blinded him and it was impossible to tell whether he had hit anyone or not. His lips thinned as he forced calm into his heart and concentrated on snapping shots at the spurting flashes of the gunmen's shots.

Crawling a little to one side, he edged around one of the boulders, forced his sight through the gloom. He could not make out the shapes of the horses and guessed that they had been tethered a short distance from the camp. A moment later there was a single shot from below and he thought he heard a grunt of pain. Then a shadow moved quickly, running from one concealing shadow to another, a dark shape that darted for the rocky ground to the rear of the small plateau.

He triggered a quick shot at the man, missed and before he could fire again the other had gone down out of sight. Straightening his body out, Ben waited tensely. The two men had evidently decided to split up and he knew that if he relaxed his vigilance for a single moment, one of them would come circling around through the rocks immediately above him while the other kept his companion covered from below. Ben tightened his lips at the thought. It meant that the girl could be in more deadly danger now. Splitting their forces could have been the wrong decision.

Turning his head slowly, his eyes now well accustomed to the darkness, he watched for anything that moved. Silence came again, but was broken almost immediately. The shot struck very close to his position and bits of rock and powdered stone stung the side of his face as he pulled his head down. The gun-flash had been further away from the spot where he had seen the man disappear into the shadows. He judged the other was working his way well back into the boulders before making an attempt to move round behind him. Which of them was it? he wondered. He did not doubt that Manvell would leave the other man to fight it out with him, to delay him, while the rancher made his getaway. Whether the other would come forward to match himself against him, he did not know.

The minutes began to drag. No further shots were fired from the rocks and Ben began to feel a little apprehension. What was going on out there? He knew that one of the men had been hit, but both had been returning his fire since then so he had not been hurt too badly.

Making up his mind, he edged back down the slope to where the girl was still crouched behind the rock. Her face was a pale grey blur as she looked up, startled, by his approach. For a moment, the rifle swung in his direction, then he whispered softly: 'It's all right, Alison, it's me, Ben.'

She relaxed, leaning against the rock. 'What's happened? Why aren't they firing?'

'I'm not sure. One of them has been hit, but the other went off into the rocks. I figured he might be tryin' the same thing I did, workin' his way around us to come up from the rear, but there's been no sign of him.' He paused, glanced reflectively into the gloom, then made his decision. 'Stay here and keep me covered.'

'What are you going to do?'

'I'm goin' in there to take a look. There's somethin' funny here that doesn't add up. Could be that they've decided to play possum and wait for us to make a move.'

'Be careful, Ben. They could be just waiting for a chance to kill you as soon as you show yourself.'

'I'll be careful,' he promised. Checking his guns, he lowered his head, then edged out into the open. Flinty rocks bit deeply into his hands and knees as he crawled forward. At any moment, he expected to hear the savage bark of a rifle and feel the smashing, leaden impact of a slug tearing its way into his body, but it never came.

Approaching the rocks, he tensed himself, edged a little off to one side and then moved over the ragged boulders. He had drawn his Colt now, and his finger was bar-straight on the trigger, ready for instant use. Lifting his head slowly, he peered about him, eyes searching every inch of the shallow plateau. At first he could see nothing. Then he made out the prostrate form of the man who lay a few feet away, his arms outflung, head twisted a little to one side.

Stepping over the rocks, he moved towards the other, the barrel of the Colt dipping downward to cover the man, ready for any tricks. The other did not move as he came up to him, went down on one knee and turned him over. The man was still breathing, but the rasping breath that whistled in and out of his throat told Ben that he had been hit bad.

Moaning a little, the other's eyes flicked open, stared up at Ben for a long moment with no recognition in them. Then his lips moved and his harsh voice said: 'You're Ben Littlejohn, ain't you?'

'That's right,' Ben said slowly. 'Where's Manvell? Hidin' in those rocks ready to plug me in the back like the snake he is?'

'He's left,' grunted the other hoarsely. He tried to struggle up into a sitting position. 'The rat shot me in the back. He's figurin' on gettin' all of that buried gold for himself. He only brought me along to take care of you if you did decide to follow us. He never meant me to get any share of the loot.'

'I guess that makes sense,' Ben acknowledged. He got to one knee, stared off into the darkness. By now, he reckoned, Manvell would be some distance away, he would have walked his mount so as to make no sound and then mounted up when out of earshot.

SEVEN

THE DEVIL'S DUES

'Do you think he'll live, Ben?' Alison Faulds asked, as she bent over the shot man.

Ben shrugged. 'Hard to say. The bullet is still in there somewhere, but we can't get it out. Even if we did, I doubt if he would live through the night.'

'Then what are we going to do with him?'

'We'll have to leave him here and go after Manvell. If we waste any more time we'll never get him.' He expected the girl to argue, maybe even offer to stay with the wounded man, but she said nothing, merely staring stonily into the darkness in the direction in which Manvell had gone.

Saunders arched his body and the stab of pain that went in a vicious spasm through him jerked his mind back from the edge of unconsciousness. His lips worked slackly for a moment and then he said jerkily: 'He's cuttin' through the hills to the north-east, Marshal, then over into the desert. I ain't got any real idea where that treasure is buried, but he did say somethin' about three bluffs close to a rocky knob out in the Badlands north of the range.'

'I understand,' Ben said. In spite of the fact that this man had tried to gun him down in cold blood only the previous day, he felt a little compassion for him and knew that he was telling the truth. Saunders had been wrong to trust Carrico Manvell from the very beginning. The other held life very cheaply. All he had ever cared about were money and power. Now he felt certain that he had the key to both of them and no one was to stand in his way.

'Just stay here and take it easy,' Ben told the wounded man as he got to his feet. 'We're goin' after Manvell. There's water in your canteen and some food too. We'll drop by this way when we come back and if you're still here we'll get you into El Angelo and to a doctor.'

'Don't you worry none about me, Marshal,' croaked the other. 'This may be the big one as far as I'm concerned, but so long as you get Manvell I'll die happy.' His voice trailed away into silence and his head slumped forward a little on the hard ground. Ben thought for a moment that he was dead, but bending a little, he could still hear the other's rasping breathing and he knew that he was still alive, though unconscious.

'Let's push on after Manvell,' he said harshly. He had hoped to be able to make camp for the night but this new turn of events made it more imperative than ever that he should trail Manvell closely. The other was still tricky and dangerous; he had shot his companion in the back to ensure that he was not around to share the loot when he found it, and that could also mean that he was fairly confident he could manage things by himself from now on.

The darkness was now complete as they rode on, through the harsh, rough country, following the narrow trail where it wound in and out around the lee of the mountains, moving up from one canyon to another. The girl made no complaint through the whole of the long night and when dawn came, to find them high in the upper reaches of the mountains, with the trail just beginning its downward turn towards the vast stretching deserts below them, he knew that they would have to rest up. The trail led downward at a breakneck drop in places and he doubted if they or their mounts could make it in their present condition.

They made camp by a small stream, born in the peaks just above them, the cold, clear water rushing in a foaming froth over the rough stony bed. Dipping his bandana into the water, Ben ran it over his face and neck, feeling it crack the mask of dust that had formed on his face, burning the scorched, tender skin beneath. Near the water's edge, their horses stood hipshot with weariness.

Once he had washed, Ben walked over to the lip of the canyon, stared down into the grey dawn, trying to make out the moving shape of Carrico Manvell, but the trail, as far as he was able to make it out, was empty, deserted.

By the time Manvell rode down from the eastern foothills of the mountain range, out towards the smooth, whiteness of the stretching desert, it was an hour past high noon and the heat was a tremendous, invisible pressure that squeezed down on him like the flat of a mighty hand. Every breath he drew into his aching, tortured lungs was a fiery lance of pain, stabbing viciously behind his ribs. His vision was becoming distorted too, blurred, his mind sickened and stunned by the tremendous glare from the alkali, as it reflected the sunlight back into his eyes. The wide-brimmed hat was no protection against this savage, reflected glare and he rode slumped forward in the saddle, occasionally rubbing the back of his hand over his bleeding face, feeling the itching mask of sand that had overlaid his flesh, biting and burning at him painfully.

As he rode, he continually jerked himself upright in the saddle for a few seconds, turning and peering back along the way he had come. He did not doubt that Littlejohn was somewhere behind him, probably very close now. It had certainly not taken the other long to find them when they were hidden up on that small plateau way off the main trail. How in the devil's name had Littlejohn known where to look for them? Was the other more a devil than a man? He felt sure that any ordinary man would have ridden on by, instead of turning off that trail just at the very point where he and Saunders had cut up into the rocks. It was almost, he thought, as if the other had a copy of the map which now reposed in his pocket; but that was impossible, of course, utterly out of the question. No, Littlejohn had followed them by mere good luck, nothing else. And that raised another question which had to be faced. Who was the other rider with him? There had been two of them among the rocks, one giving covering fire while Littlejohn climbed up onto the same level as the plateau. Yet Saunders had been certain that Littlejohn had been alone on the trail when he had ambushed him. Had one of the outlaws in these hills joined forces with the lawman? It seemed highly unlikely. Yet Manvell could think of no other explanation, unless someone had ridden out of town to help him.

As the afternoon wore on, the heat had increased in its piled-up intensity, the burning touch of the sun on his neck and shoulders bringing all of the moisture in his body rushing to the surface, soaking into his shirt until it clung to his back, chafing his body with every movement he made as he swayed in the saddle. There was no breeze to mitigate the heat. The air was still, unbearably hot as if it had been drawn through some vast oven before it had reached the desert and it was as though all of the life-giving oxygen had been burned out of it, giving him no energy when he drew it down into his lungs.

He began to doze in the saddle as he rode and at times, it seemed that he heard Charlie Monroe's voice whispering in his ear, telling him that he had no chance at all of finding the buried treasure, that he would be dead long before he reached the spot where it had been hidden.

His head would droop forward onto his chest and the movement would cause him to slacken his grip on the reins, so that the horse would jerk abruptly, bringing him sharply awake again, conscious of the physical pain and discomfort in his bruised and battered limbs. The horizon shimmered in the heat and long, invisible waves seemed to be rippling over the Badlands, making distant details shake and dance in a tantalising manner. The throbbing ache behind his eyes grew worse as time went on, like a thousand tiny hammers banging against the inside of his skull.

Through the straggling thickets and rocky outcrops beyond the last range of foothills, he followed a narrow, poorly-marked trail. Once he got out into the Badlands, there would be few, if any, trails and he also knew that any water-holes would have been long since dried up. It was now some months since the rains had come and it was only during the short rainy spell that there was any water in the desert. He had taken the precaution to fill his canteen to the brim at the last stream he had forded, but since then, once the sun had got up and the heat had risen, he had found himself drinking more frequently than was wise. His parched mouth and throat seemed to soak up the water before he could swallow it and his tongue seemed swollen to twice its normal size, moving sluggishly and rustily against his teeth. The going would be hard on his horse, but the thought of all that wealth buried near the triple buttes was enough to force all other considerations out of his mind. His brain was aflame with the thought of getting his hands on that gold and silver. This temporary discomfort was nothing compared with that.

He was descending a small, shallow ravine when the shot rang out from somewhere off to his right and he felt the redhot touch of the slug as it burned along his left arm. The flat report of the rifle came to him a split second later. He was out of the saddle, hitting the soft sand and rolling down into the ravine for cover before a further shot could come. The horse, reins swinging idly down, stood on the edge of the ravine, staring down at him.

Safe for a moment behind shelter, he pulled the gun from its holster and wormed his way forward, ignoring the pain in his arm and the warm stickiness of blood where it trickled down to his wrist, dripping into the alkali which soaked it up greedily. Peering cautiously over the lip of the gully, he strove to make out the position of his attacker. He felt quite certain that it was not Littlejohn. There was no way by which the other could possibly have got in front of him. It had to be one of the outlaws who infested this part of the territory, though the reason behind the sudden and unwarranted attack was something he could not guess at, unless they had figured that he was carrying money on his person.

Evidently there was only one man there since only the one shot had been fired and he knew the man would be hiding among the gullies nearby waiting for him to show himself again, afraid to expose himself and draw any return fire. As he lay there, he cursed the fact that he had not thought to grab at the Winchester when he had dropped out of the saddle. If the other had his wits about him, all he would have to do was circle around, out of range of the Colt and plug him off with the rifle, keeping his distance and manoeuvring to enfilade his victim.

Gritting his teeth, Manvell decided to forestall this move and wriggling back along the bottom of the gully, he moved towards a thick layer of mesquite and cactus which would afford him protection, and through which he could work his way, unseen, into the nearby gully that circled around his position. The ground was in his favour. After a burst of running, keeping his head low, he scrambled to safety in the wider gully, flopped to the bottom of it and lay for a moment, gasping air down into his heaving lungs. He was scratched and breathless, but he had already figured out the likeliest spot where the other was hidden.

From behind a tall heap of rocks, he was able to look down onto the vicious sunglare of the desert. His own mount was still standing patiently on the crest of the gully some fifty yards or so away, nibbling at the coarse tufts of grass. But there was no sign of a man anywhere around. He lay there for a long moment, scanning the alkali, particularly watchful of the darkly-shadowed gullies which criss-crossed the desert at this point. It was just possible, of course, that the other had given up the attempt to kill him and gone on his way, rather than risk a flank attack which could turn the tables against him. But Manvell was in no mood now to take any chances. In spite of the weariness in his body, his mind felt unnaturally clear. Everything seemed to be curiously magnified. It was as though he could see tiny movements much more clearly and hear faint sounds easily.

Moving stealthily forward along the arroyo, he came to the end of it, paused, then lifted his head carefully. He was just able to make out the spread-eagled figure of the man on the alkali twenty feet away, the rifle cradled in front of him, the tip of the barrel poking through a V in the rocks.

Drawing his lips back in a thin, vicious smile, Manvell lifted his gun carefully, sighting it on the other. He hesitated for a moment, then got slowly to his feet.

'All right, mister, hold it right there,' he called. 'Unless you want to get a bullet in the back,'

He saw the man below him stiffen abruptly as he called out, saw him relax his grip on the rifle.

'That's better. Now move away from that Winchester and get to your feet. I guess you've got a few questions to answer.'

He stepped over the loose rocks, moving down the powdery slope. The ground was treacherous and he almost fell to the bottom as he felt the white alkali give way under him. The man below him had straightened up, was turning slowly, hands lifting. Then, without warning, Manvell saw the other's right hand strike down for the gun in its holster, jerking it free. Manvell hardly saw the movement at all. His own gun lifted and the next instant it was spouting smoke and flame. The other jerked and grunted as the first bullet hit him, half spinning him around. The gun in his hand dropped to the dirt in front of him, exploding as it did so, the slug burying itself in the ground immediately in front of the stricken man. He put out his hands, jerking upright as more bullets smashed into him, seemed for a moment to be feeling blindly for support, then pitched forward and lay inert in the white dust.

Going forward, Manvell turned the other over with his toe. The face was one he had never seen before. He still could not understand why the other had tried to kill him; it was something he might never know.

Moving away, he heard the metallic jingle of a harness and found the man's horse tethered to a stunted bush a few yards away. Turning it loose, he took the other's canteen from its pouch, held it against his ear and shook it. It was perhaps half full. At least, it ought to keep him going until he located that gold, he thought grimly.

Going back to his mount, he hauled himself up into the saddle, the effort reminding him of the wound in his arm. Stripping off his jacket, he rolled up the blood soaked sleeve of his shirt. The bullet had cut deeply into the flesh, but had travelled obliquely, not touching the bone and although it had bled a lot, it was not a serious wound. Lacking water to spare to wash it, he rolled the shirt sleeve down again, pulled on his jacket, built himself a smoke as he pondered his position.

According to the map, he should sight the rocky outcrop of ground close to the triple peaks of the buttes in a little while. The thought roused the greed in his mind and he tossed the half-smoked cigarette away, grimacing as the smoke burned his parched mouth, giving him no refreshment. Shaking his head in an attempt to clear it, he gigged his mount forward, cast a final glance at the dead man lying in the dust, then rode north-east across the trackless wastes of the glaring white alkali.

The long hours of the afternoon paced themselves slowly by, each one an interminable, dragging nightmare to the man on the slow-moving horse. He had the feeling that he was merely a speck on the vast face of the dusty, glaring desert, that he was getting nowhere, moving aimlessly forward with no hope at all of reaching any shade. This was a part of Texas that would never be tamed. It wanted nothing of man, resisted him with every means at its disposal. It was a place where poisonous snakes abounded, a waste that a man tried to cross at his own peril. He had encountered similar places before, had ridden beside the piles of white-blanched bones that lay bleaching in the harsh sunlight, mute testimony of others who had tried to pit themselves against the Badlands.

By the time dusk came down, bringing with it a coolness that was like a benison to him, he still had not sighted the landmark for which he was looking. Had the map been wrong, or had he taken the wrong direction sometime during the long afternoon? Here, with nothing to guide him but the glaring disc of the sun in its slow movement across the cloudless heavens, it was the easiest thing in the world to loose one's bearings and go wandering off in the wrong direction. He turned to face the deep red flush that marked the grave of the sun, tried to estimate in which direction he had been travelling. As near as he could judge he had been moving north-east and should therefore have sighted the triple peaks long before now.

The first stirrings of apprehension began to twist in his mind. He rubbed his eyes, knuckling the dust from them. Sweat stood out on his forehead and ran down his face in tiny streams. Ahead of him there was a long low ridge that lifted from the eternal flatness of the alkali, running at right angles to his line of travel. He wheeled his mount a little and made it, hoping that from its vantage point, he might be able to see further than at present.

The weary horse struggled up the slope, feet sliding in the loose alkali. With an effort, it reached the top, halted of its own accord. In the pale light of dusk, the desert stretched away in front of him, unrelieved except for the gullies, filled with dark shadow which slashed their way over the otherwise smooth surface in all directions. He sat back in the saddle, defeated and full of exasperation. Drawing in a harsh breath, he held it for a few moments and then let it go. *Damn it, that outcrop of rock had to be somewhere and it would be impossible for him to miss the triple peaks. In this flat country they would be distinctive.*

The light died out from the sky as the red flush in the west faded but not before he had turned to glance behind him, spotting the faint dust cloud which hang close to the horizon. Once more, he had that uncomfortable feeling that Littlejohn was going to catch up with him before he found the gold.

The riderless horse caught Littlejohn's attention as he and the girl rode along the narrow gully, with Manvell's tracks plainly visible in the dust. Kicking spurs against his horse's flanks, he went after it, caught at the reins, then led it back to where the girl waited.

'Is it Carrico's mount?' she asked.

Ben shook his head. 'Doesn't look like it. No rifle in the boot.' He rubbed his chin thoughtfully. 'Very likely the owner ain't far away. Reckon we'd better keep our eyes open for him.'

They rode on, out of the gully and up into the rocky ground that covered the rim of the desert. A quarter of a mile further on, they came across the body of the man lying on his back near the narrow arroyo trail. Sliding from the saddle, Ben went down on one knee, felt for the heartbeat in the wrist, then let the limp hand fall onto the man's chest.

'From the look of him he's been dead for a few hours, not more,' he said solemnly.

'Who is he?'

'Looks like one of the wild ones who roam these parts. My guess is that he ran foul of Manvell. There was a gunfight and he got the worst of it.'

Alison nodded her head slowly. Her eyes widened a little and she averted her head away from the still body of the gunman, his sightless eyes staring up at the sky in a faintly accusing manner. Ben moved slowly away from the other, began to circle around, soon discovered the prints that led up into the rocks overlooking the trail.

'Here's where Manvell was,' he said finally, pointing. 'There's blood here too so I guess he didn't get off scot free.'

He swung back into the saddle. On the face of it, this looked like a chance encounter and nothing to do with why Manvell was headed into the Badlands. These wild ones were always on the look out for anybody who might be carrying gold with them and evidently Manvell had looked sufficiently prosperous for the other to try to jump him.

This encounter, brief as it may have been, would have slowed up Manvell to a certain extent and cut down his lead. The fact that he had been hit too would not make things easy for him. Grimly, he started off into the desert. He did not minimise in his own mind the difficulties which would face them out there. The long ride through the mountains had been bad enough, but here in the desert it would be a hundred times worse and again, he fell to wondering whether he had the right to allow the girl to accompany him on this last trail, or whether it was up to him to insist that she stay behind, to wait here where there would be water and shade close by until either he or Manvell returned.

Almost as if she had divined his thoughts, the girl said: 'Don't you think we ought to be moving out, Ben? All the time we're sitting here, Manvell is getting further away from us.'

'I know that,' he said slowly, evenly. 'But I've been thinkin'' and it seems to me that you'd better stay here whether you like it or not, Alison. Manvell means trouble, big trouble.'

'Are you trying to stop me from coming now that we've got this far?' she demanded. In spite of her obvious exhaustion, there was spirit in her tone and the way she straightened and sat in the saddle.

'I'm doing just that, Alison.' He did not want to have to argue with her, knew that she would match her will with his own.

She shook her head, rubbed at the dust on her cheeks. 'No deal, Ben. I said before that I'm in this to the finish and that's the way it's going to be. Now let's save our breath arguing.'

For a long moment, Ben stared at her, saw her eyes meet his, her gaze direct and unwavering. Then he sighed, nodded slowly. It was, he knew, impossible to make this girl do something she had set her mind against. Riding together, they put their mounts to the faintly-seen trail which marked the way in which Carrico Manvell had headed.

Lying on the hard rock, Saunders watched the lawman and the girl ride away, cutting through the narrow pass between the tall boulders. Gradually, the sound of hoofbeats ringing on the rock faded into the distance and the deep, pendant silence of the mountains closed in on him, with only him, with only his harsh, guttering breathing to disturb it. The pain in his back had subsided now to a dull ache which was spreading slowly through the rest of his body. He did not know just how badly he'd been hurt. The slamming impact of the bullet had itched him forward into the rocks, and he had struck himself a savage blow on the temple which had partly stunned him. Now he began feeling around with his fingers, trying to move himself. His teeth were chattering loudly in his head and he was forced to lie still for a moment in order to fight down the spasm of pain that knifed through his limbs, threatening to go beyond what he could bear and still remain conscious.

If he could only catch up with Carrico Manvell again, he would die happy. Because this time, he would make no mistake. The gun that lay a few inches from his hand would be used for its last purpose, but that would be to blast the life out of Manvell's treacherous body! He no longer felt anything towards Littlejohn. The marshal was only doing his duty according to his lights and although he had held no warmth towards lawmen of any kind, having been on the run from them since he had been sixteen and had shot down his first victim in Laredo, it was Manvell he wanted to see dead. Yet knowing the cunning and treachery of the man, he could not be sure that Littlejohn, fast as he was, would get the better of him. If he himself had only taken a little more trouble with his first shot, he could have downed the lawman back there along the trail. Manvell would not have made the mistake of hurrying himself. He would have made certain that the lawman's shoulders were in his sights before squeezing off his shot.

A retching spasm gripped him and had him jack-knifing violently on the ground. Then he twisted himself over, ignoring the pain in his back, got his legs under him and somehow found the necessary strength to get to his feet. Everything swam blackly around him for one dreadful moment and he clutched at the rocks to maintain his balance as his knees threatened to give beneath him, as though lacking the strength to hold his weight. He fought down the wave of sickness with a savage effort, wiped the sweat off his forehead and began to edge his way forward along the cut to where he had left his horse. If Manvell had forgotten to spook the animal, it ought still to be there and if he could somehow get himself up into the saddle, he felt sure he could cling onto the animal's back and follow Manvell and the other two who had gone after him.

Inwardly, he knew that he was getting worse, that there was some bleeding from the bullet wound and that once he passed out, he might never regain consciousness again. Yet he kept grimly on, obsessed by the one desire, to get Manvell in the sights of his gun and kill him, to let him know, just before he died, who it was that had pulled the trigger which would blast him into eternity.

He could feel the spasms of agony lancing through his back, low down with every movement he made; and a little voice at the back of his mind kept telling him that maybe if he made it back into town, instead of following this vengeance trail after Manvell, the sawbones there might fix him up as good as new. Then he would be in a far better condition to go after the other.

Ten minutes later, clinging to every outcrop of rock and upthrusting root along the side of the trail, he reached his horse. The animal was still tethered where he had left it. Evidently Manvell had never thought that he would be able to move again after he had planted that slug in his back. The thought brought a flush of wild elation, but it was lost almost at once in the agony that seared like a flame through him as he struggled to pull himself up into the saddle. The horse kept shying away from him, smelling the blood on his clothing, scared and uncertain. Muttering to it under his breath, he managed to calm it down and it stood trembling a little as he hauled himself up with a dizzying wrench which seemed to pull his arms from their sockets.

He lay there for a long moment over the horse's back, his arms and legs hanging limply with scarcely any feeling in them at all. The darkness of unconsciousness which lay on the edge of his vision, threatened to sweep in and engulf him at any moment, but he gritted his teeth and forced himself to hold on to his buckling senses. The urgent desire to kill Manvell was the driving force in him now, swamping out everything else. He was breathing hard and heavily, muttering harsh curses under his breath as he kicked weakly against the horse's flanks. Slowly, it began to move uphill, the swaying motion increasing the feeling of sickness in the pit of his stomach.

The main thing, he knew, was to stay m the saddle. Sweat dripped from his forehead and jaw and soaked the collar of his shirt, stung his eyes and trickled in rivulets down his dust-grimed cheeks. There was a dull roaring in his head like the thunder of a nearby waterfall and the boulders where they rose high on either side of the twisting trail seemed to be swaying around him.

Another violent spasm racked his body, arching his back and shoulders and he moaned aloud, clenching his teeth tightly together as he hung over the horse's neck. He was almost cashed in but something, some hidden reserve of strength which he had never known existed in his body, held him on as the horse moved along the trail, up to the summits of the mountains and then dipping down the far side, down towards the stretching desert which was already darkening as night fell.

Every nerve and limb screamed at him to rest up for the night, to give his torn and bleeding body a chance to repair itself, to regain some of his strength. But he knew inwardly, with a certainty that he never questioned, that once he stopped and got out of the saddle, it would be impossible for him ever to mount up again. Only the driving force of his desire for revenge was keeping him alive now. No sawbones would have given him any chance at all, would even have declared that according to all the rules of medical science, he ought to have been dead right there, that no man could survive the terrible, gruelling journey which he was under-taking. But although doctors knew the limitations of the body under normal conditions, they knew little of the innerm workings of the mind and how they could control phy ability and human endurance. Anger and revenge drive a man to do things which, in other circumstances, would have been utterly impossible for him. So it was with Saunders as he somehow succeeded in clinging desperately to the reins, his legs hooked under the horse's belly as it carried him up over the tall peaks and down the far side, moving through the long night, with the air growing colder until his limbs were so numb that it was impossible for him even to feel the pain.

For long intervals, he drowsed numbly in the saddle, some hidden instinct alone keeping him there. By the time the moon had set and dawn was brushing the eastern horizon with a pale grey, he was half delirious, scarcely able to think straight or to divorce fact from fantasy. He felt flushed one minute and shiveringly cold the next as fever gripped him. Squinting ahead of him, the rocks and trail danced and swayed so that he was unable to focus his eyes on anything. He knew, however, that he had been travelling much too slowly to catch up with any of the three in front of him. By now, if he had ridden hard all through the night, as Saunders guessed he would, Manvell must be at the spot where that treasure would be buried. A few hours spent in digging it up and packing it onto his mount and he would cut away across the Badlands, heading for the Mexico border and once over it, Littlejohn would have no jurisdiction to go after him and bring him back. Manvell had sometimes spoken of a little valley he knew south of the border where he would be quite safe from law, in any shape or form.

There was no hesitating as he rode down from the foothills. It was as if his body had become divorced from his mind, his brain no longer able to take in the fact that he was badly hurt, that with every hour that passed, he lost more blood and was becoming weaker. Somewhere ahead of him was Carrico Manvell, the man he was determined to kill before he died himself. He had submerged every other feeling and emotion to this one end.

The sun came up promising another blisteringly hot day. Saunders was aware of it, but little more. His mind had retreated into an armoured shell, was insulated now against pain and physical discomfort. His eyes were half closed, automatically, against the growing glare from the blinding alkali and he let his mount choose its own trail over the wastes that stretched out to the far horizons.

Shortly before daylight, Manvell woke to the throbbing, pounding pain in his left arm. After a while, he became conscious of the stabbing agony and sat up, rubbing the arm gently. It was swollen and as he stripped off his jacket and pulled up the sleeve of his shirt, he saw that it was badly discoloured. Some of the alkali had evidently worked its way into the wound along his flesh and had set up some irritation. He doubted if it was an infection. But his arm would be almost virtually useless unless he could bind it up and wash the alkali out of the wound. Taking the canteen which he had taken from the man he had shot, he poured the water over the long wound, pressed it to make it bleed and get the irritating dust out. The water eased the pain a little and he tore a long strip frown his shirt, using it to bind up the arm.

There was no point in trying to sleep any longer. He had not intended to sleep at all, knowing that Littlejohn must now be very close at his back, but weariness brought on by almost three days on the trail without any sleep to speak of, had made it impossible for him to keep awake and commonsense had told him that he needed all of his strength to dig for the treasure once he located its burial place.

He walked to the top of the rise, looked about him in the darkness which preceded the dawn. His mount whinnied softly from a few yards away. There was no sign of any pursuit, but he still felt uneasy in his mind. He was so close to getting what he wanted and the very idea that Littlejohn might catch up with him at this moment, almost broke him in two.

In his mind he speculated whether Littlejohn would travel through the night or not. If he had, then there was the chance that he had passed him, missing him in the darkness and was now somewhere ahead of him. Going over to his mount, he washed his mouth with water from his own canteen, letting it run around his tongue before swallowing it, He'd have to find himself some water soon, if he was to make it back to the mountains after digging up that treasure.

Saddling up, he tightened the clinch, then climbed stiffly into the saddle, rubbing his legs to restore some of the circulation which the night's chill had taken from him. Riding down the slope he pushed his sight into the clinging darkness, but could make out nothing that looked like a triple-peaked butte.

He felt a cold sweat wash over him as he figured that maybe those rumours about this map had been wrong after all; maybe it wasn't the genuine article like he had thought. A wave of anger spilled through him. Damn Charlie Monroe! He could just visualize the other laughing at him, even in death, watching him ride this nightmare trail – and for nothing!

Almost without caring, he kicked his spurs against his horse's flanks, forced it on into a quicker pace. He felt no compassion for the animal. His one urge was to find that butte as quickly as possible. Here, in the stretching wilderness, it would be difficult not to see it.

Late in the morning, with the sun burning down on him, and an utter weariness filling every corner of his pain-racked body, he rode across a scrub-topped hill and then down through a continuous thicket of mesquite and thorn, with odd patches of chapparal and Spanish sword that slashed at his horse's legs, making it rear and buck whenever they moved through the thick vegetation.

Desperately, he fought to control the animal, cursing loudly under his breath, his voice rasping from the depths of his parched throat. The sun glared at him as he topped the rise, blinking his sweat-filled eyes in an effort to see. Then he drew in a deep shuddering breath.

There, directly ahead of him and less than a quarter of a mile away, lifting from the flatness of the desert, was a triple-peaked butte with a rocky outcrop a little way off to the right of it. Without pausing to think, he kicked spurs against the horse's flanks, racing it over the last quarter mile. A faint rumble of satisfaction came from his throat.

He dismounted on the run, forgetting the pain in uis body with the urge to get at the gold. With a rising tingle of expectancy, he pulled the shovel from the side of the saddle, took out the map and checked the position of the burial place of the gold, then marked it off, pacing it out from the base of the buttes. For a moment, he stood staring down at the shallow, circular depression in the sand at his feet. It suggested that the soil had been dug away at this point, had been disturbed at some time in the past to form this notice-able sink in the level of the ground. He tightened his grip on the handle of the spade and then began to dig, heaving the sand and alkali to one side, working with a superhuman strength as if anxious to get the hole dug in the shortest possi-ble time, regardless of the effort it cost him. His arm still trou-bled him, but he forced himself to ignore it, obsessed now with the desire to get his hands on the gold and silver buried here.

The hole grew deeper over the minutes as he thrust the spade down with the boot of his right foot, heaving aside the spadefuls of dirt. Occasionally, he paused to straighten up and peer into the sun-hazed distance, watchful for any sign of Littlejohn.

How much deeper could they have hidden it? Sweat dripped from his forehead and there were blisters on his hands. Then the spade hit something hard and metallic. Swiftly, forgetting everything else, he began to shovel the loose dirt from around the edge of the hole, widening it. In the bright sunlight, he saw the glimmer of metal beneath the dirt. He continued to spade the sand aside and then the golden crucifixes, chalices came to light. Getting to his knees, he brushed the sand away carefully with his hands. His blood was pumping through his forehead, throbbing in his ears. Numbly, he shook his head, unable to take his eyes off the glittering gold and silver objects. This was far more than he had ever expected to find. He was compelled to reach out and touch them, run his fingers over the smooth surface. His hands trembled a little as he pulled them out of the loose sand and laid them out on the edge of the hole.

He was so intent on what he was doing that he did not hear the approaching riders until they were less than three hundred yards away. Jerking up his head, he squinted into the sunlight, then dived for the rifle which he had left at the bottom of the hole, ready for use. His fingers closed around it, pulled it up sharply, levering a shell into the breech. Aiming it swiftly, he got off a shot at the leading rider, saw the man jerk his mount around with a sharp, instinctive movement and knew that he had missed.

The return fire was immediate. Ducking down he heard the bullets thudding into the mound of earth near the hole, was thankful for its protection. At least he had the advantage. Those two were out in the flat wilderness where there were only a few gullies to afford them cover, while he could squat here and wait for them to make a move. There was also a little shade into which he could crawl, but pretty soon, the heat of the sun would start to fry the others and they would have to give themselves up.

'You don't stand a chance, Manvell,' called the harsh voice. 'This is Ben Littlejohn. Better throw out your weapons and come on out after them. That treasure doesn't belong to you. By rights, it still belongs to the monastery and I aim to see that it gets back there.'

Manvell licked his lips dryly. He thought fast. Maybe he could bluff his way out of this. 'All right, Littlejohn,' he called. 'But why give up the chance of a lifetime? I've shown you that this treasure does exist. It's lain here for nigh on fifty years and I figure that it belongs to the man who finds it. There are only the three of us, and a third share in this is more'n enough to set you up with a spread south of the border where you can live like a king. What do you say? We share it out equally. No sense in any of us gettin' killed over it, is there?'

'You're wrong there, Manvell. I don't make deals with any kind of killers like you. I'm takin' you back to stand trial for Charlie Monroe's death and that gold goes back to its rightful owners.'

'You're a fool,' called Manvell harshly. 'What about your friend? What does he have to say about it? Maybe he has more sense than you got.'

'We'll do just as Ben says.' called a voice.

For a moment, Manvell could scarcely believe his ears. That had been a woman's voice. For a second, he did not recognize it, then he knew who it was out there with Littlejohn.

'That you, Miss Faulds?'

'You guessed right, Carrico.'

'Now you don't want Ben to do any fool thing, do you? Like I said, this will set you up as the biggest rancher in the territory. I'm lightin' out of the country. I won't give you any more trouble around El Angelo. You've got my word on that.'

'Your word, Manvell.' There was naked scorn m the girl's voice. 'Your word means nothing to me. You're the man who gave the orders to run my father out of the territory, who ordered our cattle to be rustled and our men to be shot from ambush.'

'All right. If that's the way you want it, you'll have to come and get me. And it won't be long before that sun gets too hot

151

for you. Ever been out in the middle of the Badlands at high noon? It can fry a man's brains and blind him for life. And I'm here in this hole where there's plenty of shade and from here I can shoot you down the first move you make.' There was a triumphant note in his voice as he lifted his head very carefully until his eyes were on a level with the lip of the hole and he could just see out into the glaring sunlight that flooded over the plain. The two horses were standing two hundred yards away but there was no sign of their riders. He guessed they had gone to ground behind the animals in one of the gullies that stretched through the sand and alkali.

Stretched out in the shallow depression, Ben bit his lower lip and tried to discover some way of getting Manvell out of his virtually impregnable position. He recognized at once that there had been a lot of truth in the other's words, when he had claimed that they were at a disadvantage and he cursed himself inwardly for not having taken the elementary precaution of scouting the place first before moving in as close as this.

So long as he and the girl kept their heads down and did not try to move, they were safe from any gunfire, but how long could they stay here, exposed to the terrible, blistering glare and heat of the sun? By the time it had lifted to its zenith, they would be cooked alive. He turned his head very slowly, peering around him, taking care to move carefully and easy.

'Is there any way we can get him out of there, Ben?' asked the girl softly. There was no fear in her voice, but he saw the look of apprehension at the back of her eyes, knew that the truth in Manvell's words had struck home to her as well.

'It won't be easy,' Ben said, running his tongue around his dry lips. 'He knows that he has us pinned down and I reckon he can outwait us once the sun gets up.

'Then what can we do?'

'Nothin' but wait for him to make the next move.'

The rest of the morning passed and there was still no movement from the deep hole in the distance. Ben wondered what Manvell was doing out there, squatting down out of sight. He knew that the other had not been lying when he had said he had found the treasure. The sunlight was shining on something that burned with a pure orange-yellow glow, something which could only be gold.

Blinking the sweat from his eyes, he turned his head and looked across at the girl. Her eyes were half closed and her breathing was heavy. She had pushed back her hat onto the back of her head in an attempt to shield her neck from the direct glare of the sun, but here in the open, without any shade at all, there was little they could do in the way of getting any protection from the light and heat. He knew that they could not possibly last out the day. Already, there was a tortuous ache in his head, as if his skull were threatening to split asunder and the worst of the day was yet to come.

'Alison!' He spoke her name softly, saw her open her eyes with an effort, and turn her head in his direction. She eyed him dully for a moment, then pulled her mind back to the present, brushed a stray curl of hair out of her eyes

'What is it, Ben?'

'Think you can keep me covered? I know it's a forlorn hope, but I'm going to chance working my way around him. This glare has got to be affectin' him as well as us. Maybe I can move around without him seein' me.'

'But there's no cover at all there,' she protested. 'You'll be shot before you can get under cover.'

'That's a risk I've got to take. Anythin' is better than lyin' here waiting to go mad with the heat. Keep an eye on that hole yonder. If he shows his head, try to get him with the rifle. Think you can do that?'

Her lips moved in a brief smile. She said quietly: 'I know I'm really to blame for this mess, Ben. If I hadn't been so stubborn back there and had waited in the foothills like you asked me to, you might not have ridden into a trap like this.'

'It's no fault of yours, Alison,' he said softly. 'It's just one of those things. At least he's led us to the right spot.' Taking the Colt from its holster, he spun the chambers, checking they were all filled, then began to inch his way to the right, pressing his body into the burning sand. The dust got into his mouth and nostrils, clogging his throat, threatening to suffocate him. He knew it wasn't going to be easy to make any distance in this flat, open country, but distance was what he had to have if he was to get into a position where he could take Manvell by surprise.

Ahead of him, there was a stretch of eroded red gullies and cat-claw but the vegetation was so short that it gave him little cover. By now, he was well clear of the horses, out in the open and it only needed Manvell to spot him and he was as good as dead unless the girl got in her shot first, forcing Manvell to keep his head down.

The sun hung balanced towards noon and there were no shadows here and every few moments he was forced to pause and suck air down into his aching lungs. He was making painfully slow progress and the knowledge that he had now committed himself was a desperate urge, driving him on.

Out of the corner of his eye, he saw the sudden movement near the mound of dirt close to the hole. Desperately, he pressed himself into the sand knowing that a bullet was coming any second now. The sound of the shot made him flinch and tauten his muscles ready for the shattering impact, but it never came and as he lifted his head cautiously, he saw by the blooming of powder smoke that it had been Alison who had fired the shot.

Taking his life in his hands, knowing he would have no better chance than at that moment while Manvell was recovering from shock, he got his legs under him and raced for the rising spires of the butte. His legs slipped in the treacherous earth. He knew that he must surely have been seen now, that Manvell would risk being hit by the girl to stop him from getting to the cover of the red sandstone rocks. Lead from the hole pecked at the sand close to his heels. Turning, Ben fired wildly at the other, continuing his mad rush.

There was a momentary pause in the firing. Desperately, sucking great gulps of air into his body, everything swimming in front of his eyes, Ben darted forward, threw himself onto his chest and slithered the rest of the way towards the outcropping rocks that lifted around the towering base of the butte. Quickly, more rifle fire raked his new shelter and he flinched, grimacing as spurting slugs kicked a shower of dirt and small pieces of rock into his face. Clawing the dust from his eyes, he drew himself back as far as possible, knew with a sense of relief that he was temporarily safe from the rifle fire.

The thought had no sooner crossed his mind than Alison's rifle began firing again, pinning Manvell down, giving him no chance to try to hit Ben. It was all he needed. With all of that lead around, Manvell could not show his nose without running the risk of getting his head blown off. Plunging around the sheer face of the butte, his long legs carrying him from boulder to boulder, taking him further and further towards the outcrop which thrust out like a horizontal spire from the base of the butte in the direction of the hole that Manvell had dug, possibly a landmark which had been placed on the map as a guide, he didn't pause until he had reached it and was now less than a hundred yards from Manvell and on the opposite side of him to the girl. He was also slightly above Manvell and he could just make out the shadow of the other whenever he lifted himself a little, peering around him, frightened now, not knowing where Ben had gone under cover.

Ben bared his teeth in a twisted grin, sat down with his back comfortably against the red sandstone and pushed a couple of cartridges into the empty chambers of his gun.

At that moment, Manvell must have realized that Ben was behind and above him, for he swung round sharply in the hole, bringing his rifle about, his eyes searching desperately the higher slopes.

'You're finished now,' Ben yelled. It was still not in him to shoot the other in the back without giving him a chance. 'Better come on out with your hands lifted. This is the last chance I'm goin' to give you.'

There was a long pause. Nothing moved in the clinging stillness. Then he heard Manvell scrabbling around in the deep hole he had dug. A second later, the other yelled: 'All right, Littlejohn. You win. I'm goin' to come out. Don't shoot. Tell Alison to keep her finger off the trigger of that rifle. She wants me dead right here and now, Marshal.'

'You'll be all right if you toss out your guns first.' Ben said loudly.

He kept his finger tight on the trigger of the colt, watchful for any trouble on the other's part. Get all of his weapons away, and a rope around him, and he would still be a tricky customer, he told himself.

A moment later, a rifle came flying from the hole, landed with a soft thud in the sand ten yards from the lip of the hole. Five seconds later, two Colts followed it, and then the other's gunbelt.

'There you are, Littlejohn. I've done like you said,' Manvell shouted. 'Now I'm comin' out with my hands lifted. Keep your fingers away from those triggers. I don't want to be shot down now.'

'Come on out,' Ben ordered. He eased himself down from the rocks. He was still not sure of the other, but as Manvell came clambering out of the hole and then stood with his hands lifted high over his head, he relaxed a little, got to his feet and began to move towards the other as Manvell paced slowly to where the two horses were standing. The girl had got slowly to her feet, the rifle still pointed at the rancher, her finger still on the trigger.

As he drew closer to her, Manvell said in a harsh tone, 'Watch that gun, Miss Alison. You heard what the Marshall said. He's takin' me in – alive.'

'If I had my way, I'd shoot you down here and now,' Alison snapped. She moved towards the horses, still holding the rifle in her hand.

'Just think of all that gold back there. Enough for a king's ransom. Enough to set you and your Dad up in the biggest spread you've ever seen.'

'You don't tempt me, Manvell,' said the girl thinly. She stepped back as he came up to the horses, then flicked a quick glance towards Ben as he paused near the deep hole, glanced down for a moment at the gold and silver objects which had been piled up around the edge.

Manvell moved so swiftly that the girl was taken completely by surprise. She had seen the guns come flying out of the hole and knew that Ben was only a short distance away. Manvell slewed round, caught at the girl's wrist, pulled her sharply towards him, striking down with the side of his hand, knocking the rifle from her fingers. Grabbing her around the waist, he pushed her in front of him as a shield, holding her there with one hand, while his other hand dived under his coat, bringing out the small Derringer from the holster beneath his arm.

'Hold it right there, Littlejohn,' he rasped harshly. 'Or I'll put a bullet into her back. I mean it. Drop that gun and step away from the horses.'

Alison struggled, but it was impossible for her to free herself of his grip and the pressure of the Derringer against her back warned her how useless it was to try. Helplessly, Ben glared at the other. Then, his face grim and taut, he let the Colt fall from his fingers to the ground. He stood quite still, his hands clenching and unclenching spasmodically by his sides.

Manvell uttered a harsh laugh. 'So I've got the best of you in the end, Littlejohn,' he said shrilly. 'Reckon that you've both signed your own death warrants tryin' to stop me. I mean to have that gold and if the only way to get it is to kill you two, then I'm willin' to do that. Out here in this wilderness it's more'n likely that your bodies won't be found for months, and when they are nobody will be able to say who you are.'

'You don't think you're goin' to get away with this, do you?' Ben said thinly.

'No?' The other laughed again. 'Reckon there ain't anybody around to stop me.'

'That's just where you're wrong, Manvell.'

It was a measure of their concentration that none of them had noticed the other rider approach, the sand muffling the sound of the horse's hoofs. Ben saw Manvell stiffen abruptly in sudden shock, then he let his glance move over the rancher's shoulder, squinting up against the sunlight, at the figure that sat in the saddle, less than twenty yards away, a man with blood on his shirt and the look of death written all over his lined, indrawn features. But the hand that held the gun trained on Manvell's back was steady enough, the finger tight on the trigger, the knuckles standing out whitely under the bloodless flesh.

'Saunders!' Somehow, Manvell got the word out in a sudden croak. 'But you're dead. I—'

'No, Manvell. You didn't kill me. I swore I'd follow you and shoot you down for what you did back there. Guess I just got here in time.'

Ben saw the other sway in the saddle, saw the man's arm droop. Then he summoned up his last reserve of strength, forced his finger to press down on the trigger. The crash of the gunshot was a loud sound in the clinging stillness. Even as Saunders swayed and then pitched from the saddle, dead before he hit the ground, the slug from his gun struck

Manvell in the back, smashing the base of his spine, pitching him forward against the girl.

Alison screamed, half fell as the other collapsed forward into the sand, the Derringer falling from his nerveless fingers. Stepping forward, Ben caught the girl in his arms, staring down at the dying man. The other's lips moved. For a moment, nothing came out, then he said in a fading whisper. 'Maybe youre right, giving that gold back to the monastery. There's blood on it. Bad luck for anybody who tries to grab it for themselves.'

Ben tightened his arm around the girl's waist. She shuddered, turned her face to him and buried it in his shoulder with a little sob.

'Everything is all right now, Alison,' he said quietly. 'Manvell is finished and that means the end of the gunhawks who rode with him. In the meantime, we'd better collect this gold and take it back to where it belongs.'

Together, they walked towards the deep hole dug out of the sand, where the gold gleamed faintly in the sunlight, matching the colour of the bluffs that lifted behind them.

LOT.	EX	TH
2	6	6
19	23	13
28	38	15
33	39	25
42	43	32
49	49	(10)
(21)		